RIDING THE RIVER

STONECROFT SAGA 7

B.N. RUNDELL

WOLFPACK
PUBLISHING
— EST 2013 —

WOLFPACK
PUBLISHING
— EST 2013 —

Riding The River

Paperback Edition
Copyright © 2020 B.N. Rundell

Wolfpack Publishing
6032 Wheat Penny Avenue
Las Vegas, NV 89122

wolfpackpublishing.com

Paperback ISBN 978-1-64734-081-0
eBook ISBN 978-1-64734-080-3

Library of Congress Control Number: 2020939827

RIDING THE RIVER

1 / Reflection

The broad-shouldered young man leaned back against the pair of parfleches he had stacked behind him. It was Gabriel Stonecroft's first experience of handling a sturgeon nose canoe and he had successfully navigated the canyon through the foothills of the Madison Range and the Absaroka Range in the northern reaches of what was called New Spain, or Spanish Louisiana. Although all alone, save the big black Wolf that snoozed in the prow of the canoe, he was full of memories of the past four, almost five years. On the river for most of a day, his journey began at the confluence of the three forks that fed the beginning of the Missouri River. He came from a land little known to white men, which had only been seen by a few traders from the Hudson Bay and the Northwest companies, and of course, Gabe and his lifelong friend, Ezra Blackwell, young men that were determined to discover and explore the uncharted wilderness of the west.

The granite tipped peaks of the Absaroka range were fading behind him, the rolling foothills and plains stretched out before him with some taller timber-topped ridges off his right shoulder. The river pushed into a wide verdant valley, tall grasses waving in the breeze, with a small herd of buffalo grazing and ignoring the passing man in the canoe. Gabe shook his head, looked at Wolf who was now standing and watching the wooly beasts in the distance, "Now, don't go gettin' your hopes up, Wolf, we ain't stoppin' for no buffalo steaks. 'Sides, we couldn't fit all the meat of one o'them in this canoe!" The big black wolf, tongue lolling and eyes alert, craned around to look at his friend, as if to say, "I know, I know, but a guy can hope, can't he?"

It was the usual communication between a man and his animal friend. Gabe had the same closeness with his black Andalusian stallion that was now in the herd with the Shoshone, but tended to by his friend, Ezra, also known as Black Buffalo. This was the first time Gabe had been apart from his friend since they were youngsters running through the woods of Pennsylvania and pretending to be fighters for the revolution. It was also the first time he had been separated from his horse, his friend for almost six years. But after losing his Shoshone wife, Pale Otter, when she was stolen and murdered by a renegade Bannock war leader, Gabe had chosen to make a journey back to civilization and take care of some business of his father's estate. It would be a lonesome journey of two months or more, riding the Missouri River to the young settlement of St. Louis, but he had it to do and he was not one to shirk his duties.

He dipped the paddle into the water at the side, navigating the twelve-foot-long canoe into the main current of the slow-moving river. Although the canoe slipped across the water smoothly and quietly, he still had to go wherever it took him. The twisting, winding river often turned back on itself and Gabe could occasionally look over a spit of land to see where he was going next or where he had been just a moment ago. But he was getting used to the easy going way of the stream, smooth riding, mostly, and giving him the opportunity and time to view a lot of new country.

It seemed like yesterday that he and Ezra had left Philadelphia on their trek of exploration, embarked upon because of the threat of retaliation from the family of a man he killed in a duel. Gabe never thought of himself as a violent man, but he was a man that stood for what was right and had little patience for anyone that failed to show the due respect for others, especially when the 'others' happened to be his sister, insulted by a callous ne'er-do-well member of one of the city's prominent and wealthy families. Jason Wilson had bullied his way through life as the son of a member of the Second Continental Congress and the nephew of one of the first members of the Supreme Court. Never having to earn his own way, nor be accountable for his actions, he had blatantly insulted Gwyneth Stonecroft in front of everyone at the Society Ball, but when confronted by her brother, Gabriel Stonecroft, he demanded satisfaction in the form of a duel. Gabe accepted, and when they met, they had agreed not to draw blood, but accept the outcome as satisfaction for the wrong and both go their separate ways. However, Jason Wilson went counter to the *Code Duello* and fired before allowed, prompting Gabriel to return fire and kill the man. And when the father of Wilson posted a reward for the head of Stonecroft, Gabriel and his friend Ezra Blackwell, the son of the local minister of the African Methodist Episcopal Church, left the country, well-equipped by Gabriel's father, a former officer in the Revolutionary Dragoons and collector of weapons.

As Gabe remembered those events, he glanced down at his father's Dragoon saddle, with the holstered saddle pistols, a matched pair of French over/under double barreled flintlocks, and the Ferguson Rifle, the butt of the fine weapon showing from the scabbard. But his favored weapon was sheathed in an oiled leather case that held the unique and powerful laminated Mongol bow. Gabe had become quite skilled with all his weapons, even the Bailes double-barreled pistol in his belt, but he favored the quiet and powerful bow, capable of killing at a distance greater than the pistols, and often greater than the rifle.

He looked up to see the shoulders of sage and juniper freckled buttes pushing against the river, narrowing the bed somewhat and giving depth and speed to the current. He dipped the paddle, twisting the blade as a rudder, occasionally digging deep to propel the craft forward, and navigated past a small island that split the current. He lifted his eyes to the sky, noted the muted orange bottomed clouds, and knew that dusk was hastening its way across the land. The buttes on his left, or the west bank of the river, appeared to end at a bend that pushed away from the rolling hills and into the flats. He easily took the bend and was pleased to see the river split at a sandbar point of a long timbered island. He spoke to the Wolf, "Well boy, looks like that'd be a good place to camp for the night, don'tchu?" Wolf put his paws on the covered prow, stared ahead at the trees, craned his neck around to look at Gabe with his tongue lolling and his mouth wide open in what Gabe was certain was a smile of approval.

A narrow sandbar beckoned, and he nosed the craft toward the bank, sliding softly onto the sand. He stepped into the shallows, waved at Wolf who jumped onto the sand bar and started for the trees. With a quick look back at Gabe, a swish of his tail, he disappeared into the trees. "Oh sure, leave the work to me!

That's all you're good for, you lazy mutt!" grumbled Gabe, as he drug the canoe further onto the sandbar. He was thankful for the wolf as a companion, but every time he looked at or touched the rambunctious beast, he thought of Pale Otter, his wife that had been taken from him by a renegade Bannock. Together, they had raised the wolf from a pup since the day they found him in the cavern behind their cabin. The pup had taken to her immediately and followed her around from the first day. As he thought of her he was reminded of the smile that never failed to stir his heart, for she would look at the pup and up at him, smiling and laughing at her new husband and her new companion. He took a deep breath that lifted his shoulders and choked on the emotion as he bent to his task of making camp.

He grabbed his gear and started to a break in the trees, dropped the saddle and gear beside a ponderosa that stretched high into the waning daylight and turned back to go for the rest of the gear. Then the sudden crashing in the timber made Gabe dive for the rifle, snatch it from the scabbard and turn, one knee on the ground, to face the threat. A big mule deer buck sprang from the trees, skidded to a stop when he saw Gabe, and turned to flee into the water, but Gabe brought the rifle up, cocking the hammer as he did, and fired just as the deer turned. Red blossomed on his neck, and the buck staggered a step, then crumpled to his chest.

As Gabe rose to his feet, Wolf came from the trees, looked at Gabe then the buck, and stood with head erect and a smile on his face, proud of what he had done to bring meat to the camp. Gabe shook his head at the cavorting beast, and as Wolf came to his side, he reached down and ran his fingers through the scruff of his neck, "Yeah, you did good. We can use the fresh meat, and you'll get your share." He dropped down beside the wolf and as the canine licked his cheek, Gabe stroked his neck and head, friends showing their love for one another. When Gabe found the wolf pup in the cavern behind their first cabin, his woman, Pale Otter had adopted the animal and raised him at her side, but when Otter was killed, Wolf grew closer to Gabe and they were now inseparable. Gabe tried to leave him with his friend and his wife, Ezra and Grey Dove, as they stayed with the Shoshone village, but the wolf would have none of it and jumped into the canoe, showing himself unmovable.

Gabe stood, "Alright, boy. Now the work begins. Gotta dress out this buck and get a fire goin' for some coffee to go with the venison steaks. But first, I gotta get the other stuff from the canoe." But before moving, Gabe did as he was always prone to do, he reloaded the rifle before placing it back in the scabbard. Once that was done, he removed the packs and parfleches from the canoe, gathered some firewood and some tinder, and with flint and steel, started his campfire.

Once the flames started licking at the wood, he filled his coffee pot and set it beside the fire, then went to the buck to dress it out.

It was work he enjoyed, but every cookfire brought back images of his woman, the only woman he had loved, and it was as if she sat nearby, elbows on her knees, smiling that mischievous smile of hers that had love written all over it. But, shaking his head to clear his mind of the painful memory, his hunger spoke as he anticipated the fresh steaks that would soon be sizzling over the fire. He quickly worked to strip the hide from the carcass. Within a short while, most of the meat was deboned and bundled, Wolf was enjoying the scraps, and Gabe covered the gut pile to discourage some of the carrion eaters. He knew they would eventually find it, but he hoped he could get a good night's sleep before they began their usual fighting and bickering over the refuse.

A quick meal of left-over corn cakes, some coal baked timpsila, and the fresh strip steaks broiled over the flames, and Gabe was ready for sleep. He rolled out his blankets, using the grizzly hide atop the ground cover, and leaving the guard duty to Wolf, he sought the elusive sleep that he had been chasing for weeks. Yet every time he closed his eyes, he would relive those moments when he rushed to try to save his woman as she struggled to free herself from the Bannock. But the charging grizzly hindered him each time he relived those moments, repeatedly watching the renegade Bannock slit her throat to throw he in the path of the grizzly so he could escape. He kicked at his covers, sat up, and lifted his eyes to the heavens, asking the same question, 'Why God?' Yet he knew God's ways were above his ways and that God would in His time, give the peace he sought. But even in the times of questioning, he remembered Otter and treasured the memory.

Even when he drove those memories from his mind, he would lay back, his head on his cupped hands and look to the stars, and it was as if those memories were written in the stars for he would look to Orion, the great hunter, and the tip of his sword was their chosen star, the one she would always point out as their star. She would turn to him, smile, and say, "Our love is written across the heavens, and that," pointing to the star, "is the point it begins."

2 / Niitsitapi

Gabe had been careful. He had pulled the canoe into the brush, covered it with loose willow branches, and made certain his camp was well hidden in the trees. The cook fire had been made with long dead and dried wood, making little or no smoke, and there was nothing obvious to give away his presence. But even the most experienced woodsman can do little about the smell of wood smoke, something any traveler in the wilderness would be attuned to and cautious of, for it almost always told of an intruder in the land.

Yet with the cautions taken, Gabe slept soundly, until a cold wet nose and a low rumbling growl brought him instantly awake. He didn't move, save his eyes as he searched the area before him. A tall ponderosa was at his back and the woods were too thick for anyone to approach soundlessly. His hand gripped his belt pistol, and the other reached to his side for the reassurance of the presence of his rifle. He breathed easy as he squinted his eyes, looking for movement in the dark shadows of early morning.

Nothing stirred nor showed itself, yet Wolf still growled, a low and continuous growl, prompting Gabe to look where the wolf was focused. Through the cottonwoods that stood between him and the main channel of the river, he saw movement on the far bank. He watched, waited, listening and staring, yet not letting his gaze linger on any one thing, knowing he would see more with his peripheral vision that with a direct stare. Then he saw a mounted warrior push through the brush at river's edge, letting his horse step into the shallows and take a long drink. He held a lance at his side, a war shield hung behind his leg, the decorations catching the dim light that bounced off the ripples of the water.

Two more came to the water beside him, each letting their horses drink long and deep, but none dismounted. One had a quiver of arrows at his back and a bow across his chest, the other held a trade fusil rifle across the withers of his mount. The first to the water lifted his head, looked directly toward the trees that stood before Gabe, and moved his head side to side, obviously trying to catch the source of the hint of wood smoke. But the fire had long been extinguished and what he smelled was what lingered in the trees, betraying nothing. He spoke to the others, too low for Gabe to understand, then all three backed their mounts from the water and took to the trees.

Gabe knew he was in the heart of Blackfoot country. Even the land where he left his friend, Ezra, and the Shoshone, was at the juncture of Crow, Blackfoot, and Shoshone land, but now he was in the territory of the Blackfoot and every encounter he previously had with the Blackfoot, had been a bloody one. Yet he knew by traveling on the Missouri, he would be in their land for a few more days, it wouldn't be until the Missouri turned due east that he could put the Blackfoot behind. Although the land to the east was Gros Ventre territory, and they were a part of the Blackfoot confederacy.

He looked at Wolf, ran his fingers through his scruff as he lay beside him, "Well boy, I reckon we won't be gettin' much sleep for several days. That is, if'n we don't wanna wake up scalped!" The big wolf looked at Gabe, stretched out and opened his mouth wide as he appeared to yawn, but only groaned and dropped his head between his paws. Gabe looked at the stars, guessed it to be close to two or three hours before first light, then sat up, and stood to go to his gear. Within moments, his gear was in the canoe and he pushed it off the sandbar and with a wave, motioned Wolf in and he followed, quickly slipping the craft into the current.

They were no more than a shadow that blended with the darkness, the paddle dripped water as he moved it alongside the craft but made no more noise than the ripples of the current. He kept as close to the edge as was safe yet stayed with the swift current to make time and distance. The river had carved its way through a wide valley that lay between finger ridges that climbed to higher timber covered hills on the east, and on the west, rounded buttes and long plateaus dimpled with deep ravines made by spring runoff and summer cloudbursts. The moonlight and starlight cast mysterious shadows that moved with the rocking of the canoe, and Wolf was ever attentive to everything on shore.

The river followed its snakelike course, twisting its way through the flat-bottomed valley. Cottonwood, birch, and burr oak populated the shores, with thick underbrush of chokecherry, willow, and service berry bushes. Although the thick growth hindered Gabe's view of the valley, it also offered ample cover for his passing. The occasional clearing showed ample game as he saw a small herd of buffalo, maybe four or five hundred, two bunches of antelope, and several mule deer that returned to their beds in the trees as the morning sun blazed across the flats.

With the sun high overhead, the river was herded into a narrow canyon by buttes that crowded together at the end of the long valley. The current quickened, and the roar of rushing water ricocheted off the canyon walls to offer a welcoming chorus to the already tired traveler, but the gorge also offered escape and perhaps refuge. At least no mounted warriors would follow.

Gabe sat up straighter, took a tighter grip on the handle of the paddle, braced his knees against the gunwales and leaned into the challenge. The water crashed against sheer stone walls, splashing back into the current, waves tumbled over rocks and frothed behind. The rumble of the cascades was almost deafening, and Gabe glanced at Wolf, now spread-legged, bracing himself against the gunwales and thwarts, head above the prow and catching the breaking waves that drenched his fur. He bit at the offending whitewater as it crashed over the prow, growled at the waves that bounced off the walls, but seemed to enjoy the rush.

Gabe first used the paddle as a rudder, then dug deep to drive the craft away from the rocks, nosing it toward the chutes between the rapids. The prow dove under the waves, pushed through the wall of water, nosed into the empty air and crashed down on the far side. The river took a bend to the left and the waves forced them toward the cliff wall, but Gabe dug at the current, leaning to the low side, back paddled to pull the prow around and drove forward into the cascade, to tumble over the rapid into the backwater beyond. Then suddenly, the water smoothed, the canyon widened, and the ripples lessened. Gabe grinned, looking at a drenched wolf who tried shaking the water from his fur, "Hey!" He held up his hand to shield his face, "You're gettin' that all over me! I'm wet enough!" The big wolf craned his neck around to look at Gabe, grinning all the while as if to say, "Let's do it again!"

Gabe had lain the paddle across the gunwales as he wiped his face off, then grabbed at it and pointed the craft toward the west shore. The trees split and a grassy bank showed two people, a young boy and an old man, both native. The boy was watching the old man cast a net into the water below a large boulder that sheltered a bit of backwater. The two were so focused on the task, they had not seen the canoe, and Gabe back paddled, to move closer to the shore, seeking any cover they could find. He nosed the craft onto a narrow sandbar populated with chokecherries, then seeing they were sheltered from sight, he stepped out and pulled the canoe closer to the shore. With a wave, he motioned Wolf ashore, and bid him stay as he unloaded the canoe. Once it was empty, he lifted it over the bushes, lay it alongside and underneath the overhanging branches, tucked his gear alongside, then with Wolf beside him, he started downstream toward the fishermen.

Gabe was familiar with the Blackfoot language, although not fluent. But with his limited language, the similarity to the Arapaho dialect, and with sign language, he felt he could make himself understood. He walked quietly up behind the two as they were busy picking their catch from the net, "*Okii, knee da nick goo, Spirit Bear.*" The old man turned to stare at the white man that had come upon them silently, and that spoke his language and used sign. He understood him to say, "Hello, my name is Spirit Bear." The old man looked from Gabe to his grandson, then back to Gabe and answered in Blackfoot and sign, "My name is Walking Thunder, this is my grandson, Beaver."

"You have a good catch there," answered Gabe, nodding toward the fish. There was a pile of about a dozen nice sized trout, some still flopping.

"My grandson is a good fisherman," answered the old man, proud of his grandson.

Gabe looked at the boy who was staring wide-eyed at him, then when Wolf stepped up beside Gabe both the boy and old man drew back, looking at the wolf then at the man. Gabe dropped to one knee beside Wolf, put his arm around his neck and said, "This is my friend, Wolf."

The boy looked at the black wolf, then to the man, and back at the wolf. He spoke softly to his grandfather, "Grandfather, that is a big wolf! And the man holds it like it is his friend. Why is that?" and looked back at the pair before him.

The old man stood, looking up the bank at the man and his friend, "It is not common for us to see a wolf so close or with a man at its side. Do you have some special power that you can do that?"

Gabe grinned, "No, I found him as a pup and raised him. He sees me as his pack leader and friend."

The old man slowly lifted his head, understanding, then looked again at the wolf. But his attention was taken when the boy started toward the animal, hand outstretched. Gabe spoke to Wolf, "Easy boy, he's friendly," but kept his arm around Wolf's neck and drew him close. He watched as the boy reached out to touch wolf's fur, and then draw his hand back quickly. He looked up at Gabe with a question on his face and Gabe said, "You can touch him, but slowly, until he makes friends with you."

When the boy touched the scruff of Wolf, the beast sat down, stretched out his paws, and let the boy sit beside him. The old man watched, amazed, and looked at the white man. "We are going to have fish for our meal. Would you eat with us?"

Gabe grinned, nodding, "Happy to, where is your camp?"

The old man pointed to a break in the trees and as Gabe looked, he saw their camp. A brush lean-to sat between two young cottonwoods, and their other paraphernalia lay beside a log. A ring of stones marked their fire site and Gabe stood, "Shall I bring my things?"

"Yes. I will clean the fish. You bring your things. We will sit, eat, and talk."

Gabe grinned, stood, motioned to Wolf to come along, and returned to fetch his gear. Camp would be less lonely this night.

3 / Piikáani

Walking Thunder proved to be a talkative man. Perhaps it was his advanced years and maturity that longed to share tidbits of wisdom and memories, thoughts that often went unexpressed in the midst of familiar people and family. But the opportunity to share and remember with this man who was a stranger to the people, seemed to invigorate the old man, and he talked. As they enjoyed the repast of fresh trout, baked in the coals of the slow burning fire, it was a treat of feasting on both fish and memories.

"All this land," began the old man, waving his arms about, "is the *Niitsitpiis-stahkoii,* or the land of the Blackfoot. My people are the *Piikáani,* or the Piegan as we are called by the French traders. Those that live to the north are the *Káínaa,* or the Bloods. And west of them are the *Siksika,* the Blackfoot."

"Are not the Gros Ventre a part of the Blackfoot?"

asked Gabe, picking the tender meat from the fine bones of the trout with his fingers, then licking the juices from his fingers.

The old man nodded, "If you stay on the river," nodding toward the Missouri river below them, "you will go through the land of the *Niya Wati Inew,* They Live in Holes People, or as the traders call them, the Gros Ventre. Before my time, they were a part of the people, but the people parted, and they are no more. Beyond them are the *Nehiyaw-Pwat,* the Cree, and the *Niitsísinaa,* the Assiniboine. They are all enemies of my people." He paused a moment, chewing on a roasted turnip. The old man paused, picked at his food, and continued, "I was a chief among my people, the *Nitawyiks* band of the *Piikáani.* When I was his age," nodding to his grandson, "I was called Little Fat Worm until I took two coups by stealing a horse that was tied by the lodge of a Shoshone. I stole it to have a pony for the woman I stole. When the Shoshone warrior came after, I turned and killed him, took his scalp, and rode into my village with a scalp, stolen horses and a woman. The brother of my mother changed my name to Walking Thunder." He stuck out his chest proudly, took another trout and leaned back, "That Shoshone became my woman and is the grandmother of Beaver," nodding to the boy.

"So, you're first wife was a Shoshone?" asked Gabe, leaning forward in interest.

"Little Red Bird. When I stole her, she was very pretty, made like a woman should be," he used his hands to motion the figure of a woman, smiling and chuckling, "but as she grew old, she became fat." He pouted for just a moment, then smiled as he looked up, "But she keeps my blankets warm in the winter, and when the sun in hot in the summer, she stands behind me and keeps it from me." He nodded as he spoke, grinning and laughing.

"My woman was a Shoshone," stated Gabe, remembering Pale Otter.

"I thought so," answered Thunder, "Many of your words are like Shoshone. I thought you might have lived with them." He paused, looked at Gabe, "Did you leave her behind?"

Gabe sighed heavily, "No, she was taken by a Bannock war leader, and when I caught up to them, he saw me, then a big sow grizzly was charging, so he cut my woman's throat, threw her in front of the bear and took off at a run!" Gabe had growled the words as he thought about the one known as Moon Walker who had taken his woman and killed her.

"Where is the Bannock now?" asked the old man.

"Dead. We fought before his people, and after he was shamed, he tried to take me from behind and another buried his tomahawk in the man's head."

"This is good. This land is better without his kind," surmised the old chief. "Before I took my woman, when I was the age of this one," he nodded toward Beaver, "my people had few horses. The Shoshone, Salish, Crow, all had horses and would raid our people. My sister was taken by the Crow. But my people needed horses, so in the time of greening, we went on many raids. We took many horses, weapons, women, and scalps. It was a time when many of our young people became men. Now, the *Piikáani* are known as great warriors. We raid the Salish, Shoshone, Crow, and more. Now, we are feared!"

Gabe dropped his head, picked at his food then lifted his eyes to the old man. "I have fought against some of your people that raided in the south. A band led by a man known as Feathers and one of his warriors, Big Snake, attacked a village of women and children and old people, took the women captive and fled. We followed and took back the women. Those two got away. The rest were killed."

The old man frowned, "I heard of this battle. Feathers and Big Snake said they were attacked by a band of Shoshone of more than a hundred, and they killed many before they fled."

Gabe chuckled, "No, just me and my friend, Black Buffalo. After Feathers and Big Snake ran away, then the Shoshone band of about three hands came, but the fight was mostly over by then."

The old man shook his head, "I heard whispers of a great warrior that could shoot arrows many times farther than anyone. That warrior had many weapons, rifles, and more. He killed many of our young warriors and no one could get close to him without dying. It is said he alone killed two hands of our warriors."

"How did you hear that?" asked Gabe, confused.

"There was another that escaped that battle. He told of this great warrior. He said this warrior stopped the entire band by himself. Is this so?"

Gabe dropped his eyes, "I thought they had my woman and the woman of my friend. Those Shoshone women were sisters. But she was not a captive. The Bannock had taken her before your warriors came. After that battle, I gave chase to catch the Bannock."

For a while, the men sat silent, pondering what each had learned, then the old man spoke, "The name, Spirit Bear, how was it given?"

Gabe grinned, "A chief of the Arapaho said I should be called the Claw of the Spirit Bear. He said my bow and arrows are as deadly as the claw of the bear." Gabe reached into his saddle bags and pulled out a small bundle, unwrapped it and handed it to the old man. "That is the necklace he gave me. His father's father made that. Those claws, with the white hair, came from a Spirit Bear found in the north country."

The old man handled the beautiful necklace with great care and respect. He admired the long claws that were creamy white at the base but with glossy black tips. Each claw had tufts of yellowish white fur at the base. The red felt pad and the multi-colored coral made a stunning piece of jewelry, and the magnificent craftsmanship in the carving and shaping of silver and more accented the beauty. The old man gently folded the cloth over the piece and handed it back to Gabe.

"I have seen this Spirit Bear. We went on a raid in the land of the Kootenai and in the mountains, we saw this bear. He was the size of the grizzlies in our mountains, but we saw him for only a moment." He looked at Gabe, let his eyes linger on the dark blonde hair, then on the build of the man, and added, "The Arapaho chief has named you well."

Beaver leaned past his grandfather, "Is it true you can send an arrow farther than any man?"

Gabe grinned, "Well, the bow I use is very powerful. But I don't know if I can shoot further than *any* man."

Gabe reached for the case that held his Mongol bow and brought out the weapon for the boy and his grandfather to see. The old man scowled, looked from the unstrung bow to Gabe and back to the bow. Gabe grinned, knowing that it was something like the man had never seen. The unstrung bow lay in the shape of a "C" and as Gabe lifted it, he put his feet on the limbs on either side of the grip, then reached down to grasp the limbs and pull them back toward himself. Once in position, he carefully slid the loop of the string into the nock and the bow held its recurve shape, totally different than the typical Indian bow.

Gabe held it out for the old man to examine and he explained, "The covering is of birch, to keep the rest of the bow dry. The outer layer on the belly is of ram's horn, and on the forward outer surface is sinew. The interior is of a hard wood, and the laminated layers are held by a glue made from the bladders of fish."

The old man lifted the bow to hold before him as if to shoot, then plucked at the string, but was amazed at the strength. He pulled with his full strength and could barely move the string. He looked at the bow, then at Gabe, frowning, and shook his head.

Gabe said, "Let Beaver hold it," and the old man handed it off to his grandson.

The boy did as his grandfather did, and could not draw the string at all, but exerted all his strength and the taut string stung his fingers. He looked at Gabe with a frown, "Can you pull it?"

Gabe grinned, took the bow, and with his jade thumb ring in place, brought it to full draw using his thumb and fingers locked over the thumb. He slowly brought the bow off the full draw and put it to his feet to unstring and case the weapon. Both the boy and his grandfather watched silently. When he fastened the case and set it aside, he looked at the two and said, "I would shoot an arrow, but it is too dark to find one." He reached to the quiver and brought out a special arrow, held it out to the boy, "Ever see an arrow like this?"

The boy accepted it, looked at is unusual length, the black color of the shaft and the turkey feather fletching, but when he looked down the shaft, he saw a long hollow piece of bone attached to the shaft. He frowned, pointed it out to his grandfather, then looked at Gabe, questioning.

Gabe grinned, "That is a whistling arrow. Here, let me show you." He lifted the attached bone to his lips, blew through it as if the arrow was in flight, and a dim whistle sounded. "When that flies through the air, it is very loud. It will make a deer or elk stop in its tracks to look for the sound."

The boy was fascinated, blew through the bone whistle and was thrilled to hear it screech. He looked at his grandfather, "Have you ever seen an arrow that whistles?"

The old man grinned, "Not until now."

As Gabe put the arrow away, the old man asked, "Will you be on the river long?"

"I have a long way to go to the settlement of the white man. It will take two or three moons."

"My people are going to the gathering of nations where we will have the *Okan*, the Sun Dance. As you travel, you will see many bands as they go to the gathering and there will be many warriors on the hunt. It will be a difficult time for you. But, if you are taken, tell them you are a friend to Walking Thunder, and you will be given passage." He held out a small carved totem, carved from a piece of reddish soapstone, and was the perfect caricature of a bear. "I was told by *Napíi* to carve this. It is for you. This will show others you are my friend."

"I am honored Walking Thunder; you are a great man and your grandson will one day be as his grandfather. You will be proud of him."

"I would say you could travel with us, but you have no horse. And I cannot go with you, I do not like the water," said Walking Thunder, grinning.

Gabe looked at the night sky, stars dancing in the darkness, and the moon showing full and bright in the eastern sky. He grinned, looked at Thunder, "I will be traveling at night. I can make good time and not be seen. It is safer for one man alone."

"But you have Wolf!" declared Beaver.

"Yes, I have Wolf, and he is a good friend and he likes to travel. We have a long way to go, so," he stood and reached for a bundle of his gear. "I best get started."

"We will help you. It has been good to talk with you," stated Thunder as he bent to pick up a parfleche to help his new friend.

When Gabe lifted the canoe from the overhang of the bushes, both the old man and his grandson marveled at the craft but were not surprised. This white man had already shown them many wonders and one more was not alarming. He sat it into the water, the prow on the sandbar, and deftly loaded his gear. He turned and grasped the hand and arm of Thunder, "I am honored to have spent the time with you." Gabe looked at Beaver, took his forearm in the same grasp, "You are a good young man, always listen and learn from your grandfather."

The boy nodded and stepped back beside his grandfather to watch this strange white man motion his wolf into the canoe, and push it off the sandbar, step in, and with a quick stab of the paddle, push away. He lifted the paddle in a wave to his new friends, and soon quietly disappeared into the darkness. Beaver looked to his grandfather, "Grandfather, he was a great warrior, was he not?"

"Yes, I believe he is, Beaver. It is good for you to have talked with him."

"I have never known a man like that. And to have a Wolf as a friend," he shook his head as he considered all he had learned on this night. "Are all white men like he is, grandfather?"

The old man considered as they walked, and answered, "Like with our people, there are some that are great men, and some that are men that bring shame on their people. So it is with people like Spirit Bear, and others that are different from our people. You must learn to know the person and not the people."

The boy grasped his grandfather's hand as they walked back to their camp. He would have much to think about in the coming days, perhaps years.

4 / Contact

With the time spent around the cook fire with Walking Thunder and Beaver, Gabe found his night vision a little wanting. He took his time as he let the current carry the craft, using the paddle as a rudder and letting his eyes become accustomed to the darkness. Although the big moon did its best to light the way, aided by a clear sky bedecked with the lesser lanterns of the night, with the hills pushing in on the river, the canyon walls cast long and dark shadows.

"Well, Wolf, at least the hills are keeping the river on course. No more twisting back on itself, just pushin' on downstream." The one-sided conversation was a common anomaly among solitary mountain men, often talking to their horses or even the trees, just to hear their own voices almost as a reassurance they were still breathing. Whenever the canyon opened up to allow a little more moonlight to dance on the ripples, Gabe dug deep with his paddle, always seeking to make as many miles as possible. It had been a long day, starting well before dawn and no time of rest with it now pushing toward midnight.

Yet the nighttime was his time. Often traveling by moonlight, he enjoyed the quiet and the occasional night sounds. Whenever there was a backwater or side slough, the chorus of bullfrogs bid him travel on, and when the hills dropped their shoulders, the inharmonious choir of cicadas sang him onward. And when the banks held their depository of cottonwoods, the wise old owls would ask the age-old question of the passerby. But he often longed for the cry of the hunter of the dark, the nighthawk, the screech from high above that reassured him that he was alone on the river.

Suddenly a moving cloud of black swooped overhead, high-pitched squeals clashing with one another. Wolf jumped to his feet, head twisting back and forth, and forgetting where he was, he leapt high to try to catch one of the thousands of bats that swooped down towards him. But when he came down, he splashed into the water and started paddling toward the sandbar on the lee side of the bank. Gabe chuckled, and back paddled, pointed the craft to the smooth water and nosed into the sandbar. He spoke softly, "Alright you crazy wolf, get in!"

With a skin rolling shake, the big black wolf separated himself from the shadows, and jumped into the canoe, just as Gabe back paddled off the sandbar. Wolf looked with drooping eyes over his shoulder at Gabe, almost apologetically as he settled back onto his belly, head lifted and watching the water before them. With a side glance, Gabe spotted the black maw of a cave high up on the cliff face that had been the source of the cloud of mosquito catchers. He shook his head, chuckled at the wet canine, and pushed into the current, staying as near the middle of the current as possible.

After a few miles, the river made a wide swing back to the east and a broad alluvial plain that came from his right prompted Gabe to put in and take a brief look around. The moonlight showed a wide grey valley that stretched west to the shadowy mountains, but behind him to the east, more mountains, if they could be called mountains, stood as sentinels with the moon casting long and mysterious shadows into the ravines that showed as old age wrinkles on their slopes. Gabe stretched his legs and Wolf took off after a jackrabbit, ignoring Gabe's low-voiced commands. Gabe walked up the low rise, feeling the river-washed sand beneath his moccasins, breathing deep of the sage scented night air, and swinging his arms side to side to flex his shoulder muscles that had started to cramp up on him. He arched his back, bent over to touch his toes with his fingertips, then stood tall, looking at the serene vista before him.

The mountains caught the moonlight and seemed to shake their shoulders to awaken the creatures that snoozed in their trees and shrubbery. Gabe saw the silhouette of a couple mule deer, a young buck still in the velvet and a doe, making their way to a small feeder creek that came from the high country. He stood still, watching them tiptoe around the patches of prickly pear cactus and the skeletal branches of the cholla. They disappeared in some willows that marked the confluence of the small creek and the river. Gabe grinned, and turned back toward the canoe, and saw a self-satisfied Wolf trotting toward him with the remains of the jackrabbit dangling from his mouth.

"You look like you're happy with yourself!" said Gabe, motioning the wolf to the canoe.

He pushed it into the smooth backwater, stepped in and quickly had the craft pointed to the dark mouth of the canyon. He could hear the rapids crashing against the walls, but a glance overhead showed the big moon smiling down, lighting his way into the maw. He grinned confidently as he guided the canoe into the chutes, twisting his way between the boulders that showed like islands in the moonlit ripples. Whitewater crashed before him, but he nosed between the big rapids, sliding over the slight fall as he leaned way back to counterbalance the lightweight canoe. The nose dipped deep, but the sturgeon nose with its cover, came smoothly up, with only a side splash that washed off Wolf's dinner.

Within moments, the canyon wells moved back, and the water slowed as the river widened. The flats of the plains stretched out in the dim pre-dawn light, and Gabe sat back with the paddle across the gunwales, smiling and satisfied with his new found skill in the canoe. The river bent back on itself, winding its way past a long peninsula that pointed to a basin in the nearby hills, then with a couple more twists, another row of hills showed themselves as a barrier before the plains. But he was tired, and the eastern sky was showing grey, so when a cluster of cottonwoods stood on the east bank, he decided to make camp.

A pair of ponderosa pine stood alone back from the river bank, with some chokecherry bushes nearby. Gabe glanced at the sky, guessed there to be at least a couple hours of darkness remaining, and decided to take advantage of the remaining night and smoke the rest of the deer meat. He quickly cut some willows to fashion a drying rack, and got his fire going beneath the long branches of the ponderosa, using the long-needled pine to filter the smoke as it rose in the dark sky. He wasted little time cutting the meat into thin strips and hanging them on the rack. By the time the strips were ready, he tossed some chokecherry branches on the coals, let them start smoking and set the rack astraddle of the coals for the meat to absorb the sweet smoke. He rolled out his blankets, bid Wolf come close, then stretched out to catch some shuteye.

Less than two hours later, a low whine brought Gabe instantly awake. The grey light of early morn arched overhead, and shadows were stretching across his camp. Wolf was standing, hackles raised, fangs showing, and a low growl rumbled in his chest. A quick glance showed Gabe where the Wolf was looking and with rifle in hand, he slid from his blankets and rose to one knee, looking through the thin cover of trees to see riders approaching. Five, no, six mounted warriors, coming single file, but then they spread out, and Gabe knew they had spotted his camp, probably smelled the smoke.

He glanced down at his saddle that sat on the log, pistol holsters close at hand, and he lay the rifle across his lap, but brought the hammer to full cock. He sat back on the log, looked at his coffee pot at the edge of the coals, and reached forward to pour a cup of strong brew. His casual gaze showed the Indians had dismounted and were coming through the trees toward him, scattered out through the trees and brush. He knew that directly behind him; the thicket was too dense to allow anyone to come near and he motioned Wolf back into the brush.

Wolf had no sooner disappeared than one of the warriors that Gabe took to be the leader, stepped out from the trees to stand before him. With a stern expression, he brought his lance across his chest and pointing his chin toward Gabe, demanding, "Who are you, why are you here?" He spoke in Blackfoot, but Gabe could make out his meaning and he answered,

"I am Spirit Bear. I am a friend of Walking Thunder. I am passing through *Niitsitpiis-stahkoii*, the land of the mighty Blackfoot. Who asks?" Gabe remained seated, brought the cup to his lips and used the motion to locate the others that still held back in the trees.

"We are *Piikáani.* This is our land. You say you are a friend to Walking Thunder, how do we know this?" demanded the warrior. He was a strongly built man, square jawed, wearing a loincloth and leggings, a hair-pipe breastplate, two feathers dangling from a scalp-lock, and a long-ragged scar across one cheekbone.

Gabe held out his hand with the carved soapstone bear, opened his palm to show the carving, "Thunder said this would tell anyone of our friendship."

The warrior lifted his head and leaned forward slightly as if to look, but his eyes lifted just beyond Gabe and Gabe caught the look and ducked to the side, rolling behind the log. A scream came from behind him and the growl of Wolf as the big black beast lunged from the brush to take down one of the warriors that had come from the trees near Gabe. Within seconds Wolf had ripped the man's throat apart, and stood astraddle the body, growling, blood dripping from his jowls, eyes darting from one warrior to the other.

Gabe shouted, "No!" as one brought up his bow, ready to shoot, but the man did not stop, and Gabe swung the rifle to bear and squeezed the trigger. The blast rattled the trees as smoke belched into the small clearing and blood blossomed on the chest of the warrior. Gabe dropped the rifle and snatched the pistol from his belt as he stood. The other warriors stood frozen as they watched the big black wolf come to the side of the man, and both stood staring at the warriors. The speaker looked from the wolf to Gabe and back again, then asked, "What are you that the Wolf obeys your command?"

"I am Spirit Bear, friend to Walking Thunder."

The leader looked at the man before him, saw the grizzly claw necklace that circled his neck, then looked at the man's pistol. "You have but one shot, we are four."

"You were six, and I used one shot. Look at this pistol, you will see it has two barrels. That means I have two shots. But I only need one, that is for you."

"If you shoot me, the others will kill you," growled the leader.

"They could try. Or, you could take your dead and go back to your people. Tell them you met Spirit Bear, the one who killed two hands of warriors that rode with Feathers and Big Snake, and you lived. They will think you are a great warrior." Gabe watched the eyes of the man as they flared at the mention of their own warriors, Feathers and Big Snake. The leader looked from Gabe to the others, then to Gabe and Wolf. He motioned to the others to take the bodies of their dead and Gabe stepped aside to allow it.

Gabe watched the four warriors go to their horses, lay the bodies of their companions over their mounts, and ride back the way they came. As he watched, he quickly reloaded the rifle, checked the loads in the pistol and started loading the canoe. He was certain the Blackfoot had not seen the canoe, and he wanted to put some distance behind him before stopping again. It was just getting too crowded and he wanted some solitary time.

5 / Plains

He pushed on during the morning, making his way
through the last line of hills that rose as a barrier to
hold back the plains. But when the hills gave way to
the rolling flats, the sun was high overhead and Gabe
was still weary. The river split before him, isolating
a heavily wooded island. As he passed on the east
side, the riverbank on his right, although low, rose
about five or six feet in a sheer bank, keeping anyone
from using that as a crossing. The downstream end
of the island offered a backwater sandbar and ample
cover for a camp. Gabe swung the prow around and
pointed the canoe into the shallows, making land in
a low pool surrounded by berry bushes. But a break
in the brush showed a game trail into the trees, and
he quickly pulled the canoe into the brush, grabbed
his rifle and bedroll, and followed Wolf into the trees.
A grassy rise surrounded with cottonwood saplings

was all the invitation the weary travelers needed, and both were soon stretched out, back to back, allowing the mid-day sun to provide all the necessary warmth.

The breeze of early evening shifted, carrying the odors of a backwater slough toward the little island that harbored the lone traveler. Both Gabe and Wolf were stirred awake, Gabe lifting to his elbows in the fading light of dusk, to look around for the disturbance. He recognized the muddy smell of stagnant pond water, decaying plants, and even a hint of dead flesh. It wasn't unusual for larger animals, deer, antelope, even moose, to get bogged down in the muck and mire of a slough and be claimed by the unforgiving quicksand type bogs, their carcass becoming a meal for ravens, hawks, eagles and even the light footed coyotes. Gabe twisted around, nose wrinkling and looked at Wolf who was standing, nose lifted to the air, and spoke to his friend, "How 'bout we take to the water and find us some fresh air?" he lifted his eyes to the sky, saw the rising moon that was waning from full and guessed he had no more than a couple nights of moonlight to travel by, then it would be the more dangerous daylight travel.

The night lanterns were lit and trying to outshine one another, as the moon rose in the eastern sky. It was a clear night and a blanket of cool air hugged the ground. The canoe slid through the water like a skater on an ice pond, moving through the ripples soundlessly, its presence masked by the long shadows that fell across the water from the whispering cottonwoods that lined the shore. Overhead, the repeated *peent* cry of a nighthawk provided an escort in the stillness of the dark. The watchful eyes of Wolf peered over the gunwales, searching for any threat to their passing. Gabe grinned, dipped the paddle deeply, and pushed the canoe onward.

It was a beautiful night. A night to be enjoyed and appreciated and Gabe reveled in the mystery of the darkness, and the promise of the coming dawn. The river continued on its serpentine course, often bending back on itself, as if offering the passerby a glimpse of both sides of the landscape. Although by a winding course, the river moved north east, catching feeder creeks and all they held to add to the depth and current of this river of rivers. Mid-stream islands grew monotonous, each holding thick shrubbery and cottonwoods, and more.

Gabe found it easy to stay in the current and let the water do most of the work, but not one to sit idle, he continually pushed himself to make time. Choosing not to stop on such an easy traveling night, he surprised himself to look heavenward and see the moon nearing the western horizon. And when an unusual sound came from downstream, he lifted his paddle and sat quiet to listen. The crashing of water from below told of a hazard that would be best met in the daylight. He looked toward the shore and spotted another long island that parted the waters and offered a long sandbar. He nosed the canoe toward the shallows and was surprised to bottom out sooner than expected. He touched bottom with his paddle, stood and looked about, then motioned Wolf out as he stepped out. The sandbar fell away closer to the tree line, but Gabe drug the craft, now moving easily without the weight of both Wolf and Gabe, over the flats to a break in the trees. He pulled the canoe ashore to see what showed as a thick cluster of tall maple and oak trees that offered shade and shelter under their wide stretching limbs. He unloaded the canoe, carrying his gear to the trees, then slipped the canoe behind the tree line, and broke some branches to camouflage the craft.

With a quick look around in the grey light of early morning, he gathered an armload of dry firewood and with flint and steel, started the fire, nestled under the big branches of the trees. He was anxious for some coffee but wanted to make some biscuits in the dutch oven and needed some coals for that. Within a short while, he had a stew of smoked venison, cat-tail shoots, and camas roots simmering and the dutch oven with cornmeal biscuits made from the last of his cornmeal sitting atop some coals, with more coals on top of the lid. He sat back, anticipating a feast of goodness, before he hit his blankets. But this would be a short-lived sleep, the roaring rapids below would need a good survey before he took to the water in the canoe.

The warm sun that stood straight overhead
brought him awake. He looked around for Wolf, saw
him dozing in the shade, and then slowly scanned the
entire camp. He rose, rifle in hand and gave a good
look-see round about, then a snap of his fingers
brought Wolf to his side. They crossed the narrow
island, waded the shallows to cross to the north bank
and started downstream, following the course of the
river off his right shoulder. Although he still heard the
sound of what he presumed were rapids, it wasn't as
clear and noisome as before, but he also knew sound
was more easily carried in the darkness. In just over
a mile, they neared the cascades that thundered between rock-strewn banks. He stepped to the edge and
looked over to the water. The Missouri was just over
a hundred yards wide here, and the water showed
deep, green and clear as it passed over a wide span
of water worn granite. The stone showed pale grey
beneath the water, shallows revealing the stone and
chutes cascading over sheer drop offs into thundering
water falls that stair stepped in increments of ten feet,
give or take, dropping the massive volume of water
into time worn pools that held the white water and
foam only momentarily before letting slip the fleeing
waters to take refuge in the deeper pool that showed
a number of sizable cavorting trout.

It was a beautiful but terrifying sight. Gabe knew
there was no way he would dare attempt to navigate

the canoe over these falls and rapids and expect to live through it. He would have to portage and that would take considerable effort. He looked at both banks, seeking a good location to beach the canoe and start the portage process. He chose a spot on the far bank, on the south side of the river, that showed shallows in the wide bend and ample trees and brush for cover, but clearance enough to make way with his gear and to carry the canoe. With a wave to Wolf, he started back to the island to start the process, with ample daylight to make it past the falls.

Within a short while, he was nosing the canoe into the shallow and the sandbar. He stepped out, dragged the canoe further up the sandbar and began the process of carrying his gear. He slung his rifle and scabbard over his back, then picked up the panniers and started making his way. His third trip saw him carrying his saddle, bags, and bedroll, with the blanket covering the saddle. On the last trip, his hackles had raised, and he felt something was amiss, but saw nothing and after pushing his gear into the bushes, he started back for the next load. Now he stepped carefully, his rifle still at his back. He had dropped his tunic over his belt to obscure his belt pistol, and the blanket covered the two pistols holstered at the pommel of the saddle. But all were readily accessible, if needed.

He pushed through the trees and the chokecherry bushes to where the rest of his gear was stashed but was brought up by the presence of a scruffy looking, bushy faced semblance of a white man. He stood spread legged, grinning, tobacco juice spilling onto his beard and stained teeth, what there were of them, showing through the overgrown whiskers. A big man, he resembled a whiskey barrel in build, but when he laughed, his girth bounced and showed his middle was more fat than meat. Three others, all native and probably Blackfoot, stood near the big man, one with a lance, two with arrows nocked on their bows but with them lowered. The big man appeared to be trimming his dirty fingernails with a sizable skinning knife.

"So, mon ami, I see you have much goods. We are grateful for these," he waved his hand toward the stack by the bushes, and to the gear still held by Gabe. "We were getting a little low on supplies what with no place nearby for trading, so, thank you for saving us the trouble." He laughed, his belly shaking like the bulbous belly of a jellyfish that Gabe had seen when he crossed the Atlantic. "Now, if you will just set my new saddle down, then give us your rifle, maybe we will not feed you to the fishes!"

Gabe looked around, knowing Wolf had taken to the trees and had not shown himself. He looked at those before him, calculating what his moves would be, and what Wolf would do, then let a slow grin cross his face as he looked at the grubby French man. "Oh, I don't think so. You see, I am not alone, but even if I were, I have become pretty attached to my things, and I'm not about to just give them ..." In one quick move, he released his grip on the saddle, snatched the two pistols from the holsters as the bundle dropped to the ground, and went to one knee. He cocked the hammers as he drew them and brought them up toward the two with their bows and dropped the hammer on them both. The pistols roared in unison, spitting great clouds of whitish grey smoke that carried two messengers of death to meet their targets. The two warriors were lifting their bows but too slow to stay the lead balls that crushed their sternums, pushing them back a stutter step, as they crumbled to the ground.

In the next instant, Gabe brought the second hammers to full cock and swung the pistols toward the astonished French man who was grabbing at his belt for a pistol, but Gabe let both hammers fall and the pistols barked again, enveloping the fat man in the powder smoke and the bullets blossomed red on the chest and belly of the big man, who looked down at his bulk, saw the blood and lifted his eyes to Gabe, fear and anger showing as his eyes flared, and the man fell forward on his face.

At the first blast of the pistols, the black form came from the shadows and with fangs bared, eyes blazing orange, he crashed against the lance bearer, eliciting a scream as he stared at the open maw of the big wolf just before the beast swallowed the man's face in a growl that muffled the warrior's last scream. When the man's body hit the dirt, Wolf released his grip, and spun around to make another lunge, but the man's hands were at his face and he was choking on his own blood. Wolf bit into his arm, ripping flesh away and jerking the man's body as he tried again to scream. Then with a snarl and a growl, Wolf leapt for the soft belly, and ripped it open, dragging entrails with the flesh as the man tried to kick and cover his waist with his arm, but the blood and gore flowed and within seconds, the man shivered and died. Wolf stepped back, blood dripping from his jowls, and with a deep chest inflating breath, he walked past the carnage to go to Gabe's side.

6 / Portage

After reloading his weapons, he jammed the pistols into the saddle holsters and hung the rifle over his back on the sling. With a glance to the dead, he decided to leave the others where they fell but knew he had to drag the bulbous body of the fat man out of the way and into the bushes. It wasn't out of respect, as far as he was concerned the bodies could lay where they were and provide a few meals for the carrion eaters, but it would be too difficult to step over the body as he carried the canoe to complete the portage. He stood up from the strenuous task, looked below to the inviting water, and started back up the trail to the waiting canoe.

With the canoe inverted and resting on his shoulders, he navigated his way through the trees and brush, side-stepping down the steeper part of the river bank to the rocky flat at the shore. He made the necessary trips to bring his gear and get it loaded, then with a short break as he stood looking at the stair step cascading waterfalls, he pushed the canoe into the water, waved Wolf in and stepped in and seated himself in the stern, Wolf in the prow.

He followed a shallow channel to get to the main current and once there, relaxed and using the paddle as a rudder, looked around. The near bank was lined with limestone and granite faces, with a break between the taller and lower level, and the rim rock at the top edge. The flat top stood about a hundred sixty feet above the river level and appeared to shoulder the river for a couple miles. On the far side along the north edge, the flats appeared to gradually slope down to the river level, with the crest of the slope about a hundred feet above the river and stretching about a quarter mile back before rising to the flats. The land around prospered with bunch grass, gramma and buffalo grass and the ever-present variety of cacti and occasional clumps of sage, greasewood and rabbit brush. It appeared somewhat desolate until a closer look showed the abundance of grasses and shrubs that appealed to the buffalo, antelope, mule deer and the occasional desert bighorn.

As they pushed away from the stair-step falls, the rumble and crash of the cascades faded behind them, and the current carried them lazily past a couple of long skinny islands on their north side. More greenery showed on their right and Wolf watched the trees for game. When he saw a nice sized mule deer buck lift his antlered head from the water to stare at the unusual objects in the current, Wolf turned excitedly to look at Gabe, as if to say, "Shoot him! Shoot him!" But Gabe just grinned, "No, we don't need any meat. Just sit easy and enjoy the ride." He dipped his paddle to push past the buck, but the deer jumped back and in just a few hops disappeared over the top edge of the bank. Gabe shook his head in wonder at the agility of the amazing animal.

The river took a dog leg bend to the right and Gabe kept to the center, letting the current do most of the work. They had gone about a mile when the river bent more to the right and Gabe was surprised by both the crashing of cascading water and the rising mist that showed they were approaching a waterfall, and apparently a big one. He noticed a long slough at river's edge on his left that ended where the bank of white clay and calcite rose. He back paddled, looking at the long white bank that apparently ended at the falls, then to the south bank that showed a long line of cat-tail bogs and a rocky bank. With a quick glance over his left shoulder, he began furiously back pad-dling against the quickening current, working his way to the point of the slough and the rising white bank. As he side-slipped across the current, he made a little headway and saw a break in the bank that showed a gulley holding greenery that looked inviting.

With a lot of effort, contortions, back paddling and thrusting forward, he finally negotiated the craft across the boggy slough and into the mouth of the gulley. He pushed it as far into the grasses as possible, then motioned Wolf out and stepped out onto an uncertain clump of grass but managed to find enough clumps to bounce his way to shore, canoe in tow. He sat down to catch his wind, then pulled the craft from the bog, secured it to some brush and slipped the rifle from the scabbard to make a scouting trip along the shore toward the falls.

An easy walk of about a half mile brought him to an overlook of the crashing falls. Where the river bed was usually about three hundred to four hundred feet wide, at the falls it spread out across the flat reddish-purple rock to about twice that width, forming almost a straight line drop off and the wider canyon stretched the water shallow across the rocks. He guessed the water fell about thirty feet, give or take, into deep pools that stretched across the canyon bottom. Then a variety of rivulets offered narrow escapes to the pooled water and cut the rocks and gravel to find its way to the lower reaches. Gabe looked around and saw much of the soil had the same color, as did the rock face on the far side. The sheer walls bent into a stony rainbow faced with grey, purple, blue, green, red and brown that curved to the north to force the river's course to turn to the northeast.

He walked across the broad peninsula point above the water, and about a third of a mile downstream, another waterfall dropped the river into a deep pool of still water. But these falls were at the end of the broad rainbow of rock that formed the canyon wall and were at the shear drop-off of an irregular face of the almost white limestone riverbed. Here the river seemed to trickle through several narrow channels to find the easiest cut to make the leap into the pool. But most of the riverbed carried some water, even though mostly quite shallow. Gabe looked at the sun, recognizing he had plenty of time, but he had his work cut out for him. He motioned to Wolf to follow and as he looked down at the broad back of the big wolf that stood almost waist high on him, and he frowned as he thought. With a grin, he made his decision and broke into a trot, Wolf happily keeping abreast of the man.

At the canoe, he unloaded and stood looking at the assortment of gear, calculating. Wolf was sitting, watching and waiting, unknowing of what Gabe was thinking. Finally deciding, Gabe sat the saddle and the grizzly pelt aside, lay the two parfleche and bedroll together, thought another minute, then snatched up the long rawhide and motioned Wolf to his side. Although Wolf was uncertain what was happening, he twisted his head around to get a better look, looked at Gabe, and bit at the rawhide a couple times. Once Gabe was finished, he stepped back, looked at his handiwork, and smiled. Wolf had a parfleche on either side, the bedroll lengthwise down his back, and all secured with the rawhide. Wolf sat down, twisting to look at his packs and back at Gabe, and watched as Gabe picked up the rest of the gear, swung it over his back, and with a motion, the two started out.

It was right at a mile to the point below the second falls that Gabe chose to put back in, and they made it in good time. Once again, Gabe dropped the gear near some brush, relieved Wolf of his pack, but this time, he left Wolf to guard the gear. His round trip to bring the canoe was accomplished in less than a half hour, and they were soon back on the water.

Two miles downstream, they came to some rapids that stretched across the river, and fell a few feet, but Gabe chose to try to negotiate these without a portage. He spotted a smooth chute between a couple knobby rises and pointed the canoe through the slot. The craft hung suspended for just an instant, then the nose dropped and the canoe rushed between the boulders, nosing through the crashing waves, bounding up to lift the bow into the air, then down again, slipping away as if pushed by some unseen force. Wolf had dropped to his belly, caught part of the wave in his thick fur, and when the current smoothed out, he trembled to stand, looked over his shoulder at a grinning and slightly wet Gabe, then shook violently to rid himself of the excess water, splashing Gabe and the gear that was protected under the oil cloth ground cover.

"Wow! That was a ride, wasn't it!" he proclaimed as he knifed the craft through the smooth water. But

his time of rejoicing in their brief but fun accom-
plishment was soon cut short by the roar of more
rapids coming from around a wide bend, less than
a mile downstream. He immediately started looking
for a place to put in, not wanting to try anything that
sounded that fierce.

His scouting trip revealed another river spanning
falls, but this one was more of a long cascading rapids
that crashed over a limestone formation that appeared
to be a conglomeration of water worn boulders. But it
was more than he wanted to attempt, so he resigned
himself to another portage. As they carried the gear,
he looked down at Wolf and declared, "This is the
last time we do this today! We're gonna find us a
nice grassy camp and get us a good night's rest, after
we get us a good meal. What say, boy? You ready to
eat?" Wolf looked at Gabe, grinning, tongue lolling,
and Gabe was certain he understood every word and
agreed wholeheartedly.

They made camp below the falls on a bit of a knoll
that overlooked the water and offered ample cover.
Dusk was just beginning to drop the curtain when they
got the cook fire going and the water on for coffee.
With the last of the fresh meat hanging to broil over
the flames, and some camas root in the coals, the two
friends sat back, Gabe on the log and Wolf beside it, to
await their evening feast. The sound of the water was
soothing, but would also mask any sound they would

make, but also any sounds of predators or others that might approach the camp. Yet Gabe was confident in the watchfulness of the big wolf and anticipated a good night's rest after the day's long work of portaging. He looked at Wolf, "I'm hopin' we're done with these falls, but there's just no tellin'. I'm purty sure there's gonna be rapids and such, but that canoe handles purty easy." He remembered his earlier adventure and chuckled to himself, then as an afterthought, he knew he would have to be mighty careful, for they had a long way to go to get to St. Louis and he didn't need to be making unnecessary adventures!

7 / Storm

The cloudless blue arched overhead, the bright sun bouncing lances of gold off the ripples in the water, and shadows danced about on the scarred terrain that had been carved in eons past by the ancient river. One day past the last of the falls, Gabe had navigated a series of rapids, gaining expertise with each encounter, and made camp on a narrow bar on the west bank that held a variety of trees, shrubs, and grasses. He had climbed from his camp to the flats above the river, and with his scope, surveyed the flat land for miles about. Everywhere he looked, the land appeared as a flat canvas, carved into an intricate pattern of interlaced ravines, gullies, and coulees that all fed into the greater Missouri basin. The passage of time had scarred the land by the rainfalls and snowmelt finding the path of least resistance to escape the desolate flatlands to feed the great river. It was a fascinating terrain, seen only from the highest point that lifted the watcher above the riverbed to view the broad panorama.

As he slowly panned the vista, Gabe spotted herds of antelope grazing, heads bobbing up and down, most looking toward the designated watcher, but all enjoying the green tidbits, grasses and flowers that decorated the vast plains. To the east of the river and on a broad flat, a carpet of dark brown slowly moved across the undulating prairie, leaving behind a tilled soil trail made so by the thousands of deep digging hooves of the wooly bison. An occasional movement caught Gabe's eye as an ambitious coyote gave chase after a speeding jackrabbit. But his attention was captured nearby when a little burrowing owl came from his underground haven and stared wide-eyed at the strange intruder. Wolf lay belly down on the far side of Gabe, but he lifted his head to look over the back of the man, startling the little owl to retreat into his hole. Gabe chuckled, and resumed his survey of the terrain.

Although dusk was laying its blanket across the plains, when he took a last look around he was surprised to see a long line of riders on the flats across the river. He focused in on the group, recognizing them as a band of Blackfoot, probably traveling to the gathering of nations to celebrate the *Sun Dance* as told about by Walking Thunder. He had told Gabe he would probably see some groups traveling to the gathering, but this was his first sighting of a band. He guessed there were close to a hundred, give or take, of all ages and genders. The Plains Indians always moved with their lodges and possessions utilizing the travois to carry the heavy hide lodges and more. As he watched, the leaders took the band to a trail that dropped into a ravine that led to a wide peninsula flat that pushed far into the river bottom and offered ample grass and more for an excellent campsite. Gabe scanned that area, moved back upstream where he was camped, and was satisfied his camp could not be seen from the chosen site of the Blackfoot.

He looked to Wolf, "Well boy, we might as well go back down and fix our supper. We might be here a day or two until they move away from the river. Don't wanna have to fight our way through!" He crabbed back from the edge of the bluff, stood and took to the same trail they followed to the top of the butte. Once back in camp, he walked to the river's edge to look toward the camp of the Blackfoot and satisfied they could not be seen, he began preparing his evening meal.

***

It was early morning when he rolled from his blankets. After a restless night, he had decided he would not wait for the band below to move but would take to the river before first light and hopefully be past the village before they were moving about to spot him on the water. He

didn't take time for his morning coffee, finished loading
his gear and pushed into the water by the remaining
starlight and the dim grey of early morning light.

The canoe knifed through the still water, Gabe
dipping his paddle noiselessly as he pushed into the
current. The river was about a hundred yards wide,
and the main current was to the right of center as
it began to arch around the wide bend that marked
the flat finger of land holding the encampment of the
Piikáani Blackfoot. The shadowy lodges, many with
thin wisps of smoke curling from the smoke flaps,
stood with blanket covered entries all facing toward
the east and the river. As the current pushed toward
the high bank on the right, Gabe glanced to the
sandbar of the point and saw two women, apparently
fetching water for their cooking, but both stood, and
he heard them speaking and pointing toward him.

Gabe chuckled for he knew the sight of a big black
wolf in the prow of a passing canoe would be somewhat startling, and with a bushy faced white man
making it more unusual. Gabe called out, "*Okii*" which
was a typical Blackfoot greeting similar to an English
"*hello!*" He waved his paddle, then dug deep to move
into the shadow of the high bank that rose almost
three hundred feet above the river. The long shadow
stretched across the river, masking his presence as
he paddled, first one side, then the other, moving the
craft quickly around the bend. When he looked back,

the women were still standing, watching, and as he emerged from the shadows, they waved. He was well past the bend and would be out of sight before they could sound an alarm, but he doubted they would. The river carried him around another point of flat land, and bent back to the right, completing the 'S' curve and took him well out of sight of the village.

Another two days on the water brought Gabe to the long-anticipated bend that changed the course of the river. Since his departure from the three forks and the headwaters of the Missouri, he had been traveling north by north east. But the big bend arched around and pointed the big river to the east by south east. He knew this would take him into the land of the Gros Ventre, a people that were loosely allied with the Blackfoot, but in the past had been a part of the Arapaho nation, and still spoke the same language. They were known to be a friendly people, and Gabe was hoping for a peaceful passage through their territory.

Explorers of unknown lands would always question anyone that had gone before them. With few maps available, and most of those unreliable, it was the habit of early adventurers to inquire of anyone, native, traders, and others, that had been in the land before them. Gabe had questioned a pair of trappers that had traveled with the Company of Explorers and Discoverers and the Northwest Company, that had spent the winter with the Kootenai people and traveled through this country on a trading expedition, and remembered every tidbit of information they shared. After his meeting with Alexander Henry at the three forks where he traded for the canoe, he had questioned them about their travels through the lands of the Blackfoot, Gros Ventre, and Assiniboine. And with his knowledge gained from the Shoshone, he was not unfamiliar with the river he now traveled. He knew that the big bend marked the entry into the land of the Gros Ventre, and the confluence with a sizeable river that came from the north and carried murky water, he would enter the land of the Assiniboine. He also knew it would take about a week's travel to pass through the land of the tribe also known as *A'aninin* or "Clay People" although Gros Ventre was French for "Big Belly."

It was late afternoon when he made the big bend and now eagerly pushed to the east, anxious for a camp site and a good meal. After the big bend, the river straightened out for a mile or so, made a few bends to the south, then a wide bend to the east. Here the river seemed to cut deeper through the land, the hills rising three to four hundred feet above water level and showing a wide band of white about half way up the face. He pushed on until dusk threatened when the hills were pushed back, and the riverbank offered a stretch of alluvial flats with trees and willows for cover. He accepted the first invitation, nosed the craft into the grassy bank, and soon had a cook fire going and Wolf had given chase to a rabbit.

***

When they pushed off at first light, Gabe noticed a muddy stream feeding in from the south and coloring the river water. He knew it was probably from a rainstorm back to the south as he had heard distant thunder the afternoon before, but he hadn't thought much about it. He pushed the canoe into the middle of the current and glanced occasionally at the long brown streak that held to the south bank, coloring the river about a quarter of the way across the current. The muddy water stayed with them for about four or five miles before it dissipated, but then Gabe heard the low rumble of distant thunder.

The rising sun painted the hillsides and bounced its brightness off the water as Gabe paddled directly into the rising orb. He ducked his head to shield his eyes with his brow, but the reflected sun was just as bright as the direct glare, yet he continued on and was suddenly surprised when the sun seemed to take refuge behind some gathering dark clouds. Gabe lifted his eyes and saw the thin lace trailing the dark clouds and knew that told of rain, and from the looks of it, heavy rain and maybe even hail.

The crack of lightning that sent its ragged tail to the ground caught Gabe's attention, and he began to count. When the thunder rolled across the heavens, he knew the storm was probably three or four miles away. Another silver lance drove into the ground and the heavy rattle of thunder soon followed. The wind was picking up and the water stirred into small waves, all pushing against the thin walled craft. The thought of a good rainfall didn't seem threatening, but the wind and waves caught his attention, yet he pushed on, wanting to make time. Wolf craned around to look at him, and Gabe responded, "It's alright boy, we might get wet, but both of us could use a bath. If it gets too bad, we'll put in and find cover."

Yet Gabe knew this type of terrain and knew that all the dry gulches that fed into the Missouri could easily and quickly fill to overflowing and crash into the river carrying all manner of canoe wrecking debris, as well as a wall of water that could easily capsize the craft. As he considered that possibility, he began looking for an escape. But every lowland was made so by earlier floodwaters that carried the silt and soil to the river, piling up to form the alluvial flats. He would need cover and high ground.

Another crash of lightning was quickly followed by the earth-shaking roll of thunder and he knew he was running out of time. Then a shoulder that held a smattering of juniper and cedar standing at least a hundred feet back from the river bank and maybe sixty to seventy feet higher caught his eye and he wasted no time nosing into the bank. The craft had no sooner pushed into the sand, than a sheet of rain pelted down. Gabe and Wolf jumped out, Gabe grabbing the craft and pulling it higher. He snatched the saddle and ground cover out, dropped it to the side, then lifted the parfleches and bedroll, slipped them under the ground cover, and started up the slope with the canoe at his side. Wolf took to the trees, and Gabe struggled up the slope, dropped the craft on the uphill side of a line of juniper, then slipped and slid down the slope to retrieve his other gear. The rain pelted down, and he went to his knees more than once on the slick adobe slopes, but shortly had all the gear under the trees. He found a spot under a pair of juniper, grabbed the ground cover up, tipped the canoe upside down over the other gear, and with the grizzly pelt and ground cover, returned to the trees. In short order he had a lean-to shelter secured to the branches, the pelt stretched out on the dry needles and cones of the juniper and rolled out his bedroll. He stretched out next to Wolf but separated himself from the wet coat with the blankets and settled in to ride out the storm.

8 / Distance

Everything was damp. What wasn't waterlogged and dripping, was at least wet. Dry firewood was nowhere to be had, and the only consolation was the sun was up and doing its best to warm things up a mite. Gabe busied himself packing his gear back to the river's edge and was solaced a little by the warmth of the sun and his activity drying out his buckskins. The river was muddy and roaring and when Gabe and Wolf pushed into the current, he knew he was going to be busy fighting the current and the floating snags and debris. Yet it kept him busy and focused and they made good time.

This was a wild land they passed through; ancient hills carved by millennia of storms just like the one just passed, barren and brown, seldom freckled with cacti and sage, occasionally supporting juniper, cedar and piñon. Even the game was skittish as they scrounged for sustenance or fled from equally hungry predators.

But even this land, wild and seemingly empty, grew monotonous. The river bottom shifting from narrow canyons to flats that held bouquets of greenery, only to give way to more desolation.

Two days brought them to a sudden change of direction, first to the south, then around a point and back to the north before stretching out due east again. It was at the southernmost point of the dip that the big river from the south emptied into the Missouri and Gabe thought, *That's the river from the south, now the next point will be when the murky waters from the north drop in, and that'll put us into Assiniboine country.* Four more days and they saw the murky water flowing from the river on the north bank of the Missouri. It was late afternoon and the terrain had changed, the river slowed, and Gabe relaxed, no longer fighting the current as he had for days. Although the river still shadowed the hills on the south bank, the north bank opened into the vast northern prairie land. At the confluence of rivers, the land was fertile and green, as testified by a vast herd of buffalo that covered the land like a blanket of brown wool.

Wolf stood in the prow of the canoe, looking at the herd and looked over his shoulder at Gabe, his tongue lolling and drool dripping, and Gabe chuckled, "Yeah, I know. A nice thick hunk of buffalo steak would sure taste good about now, but, what're we gonna do with the rest of it?" The expression on the face of Wolf showed little concern for 'the rest of it' for he was only concerned with the best of it. It was then that Gabe spotted a small encampment of three tipis, just back from the north bank and nestled in a cluster of tall cottonwoods. It was unusual to see such a small number, but Gabe also knew it was not unusual for the villages to split up and use smaller groups for hunting. When he saw a young woman and a boy at the water's edge, he called out "Aho!" and lifted his paddle in greeting. The woman stood, staring, then bent to speak to the boy and sent him back to the camp. The woman waited as Gabe nosed the canoe into the grassy shore, but when she saw the big wolf stand up in the prow, her hand went to her mouth and she stepped back a couple steps but stayed.

Gabe stepped from the canoe, waded the shallow water and motioned Wolf to jump out, but stay by his side as he pulled the craft on shore. Gabe slipped the rifle from the scabbard, cradled it in his left arm and started toward the woman, right hand held up, palm forward. As he neared, he spoke in sign, "I am friendly. Are you Assiniboine?" To say Assiniboine, he used the sign for stone Sioux, which was the meaning of the name.

The woman spoke in French, "Oui, we are Assiniboine. I am Carries Her Kettle, we are of the village of Crazy Fox, of the *Wadópahna Tuwa* band of the Assiniboine."

"I am Spirit Bear, this is my friend, Wolf."

"I have never seen a man that is a friend of wolves."

"Are your people hunting the buffalo?" asked Gabe, motioning to the herd in the open plains beyond their camp.

"We came to hunt, but many of our people are sick and cannot hunt. There were more, but when these became sick, the others left. After they left, the *tatąga* came, but we cannot hunt them, our warriors are sick."

"Should I speak to Crazy Fox about hunting?"

"Our chief is with the others. Our leader is Buffalo Hip, but he also is sick."

"If I kill a buffalo, or more than one, would you share it with me? There is too much for just me and my friend, and I am traveling down river."

Carries eyes flared wide as she nodded enthusiastically, "Yes. There are two other women and two boys who would help with the skinning."

Gabe grinned, relieved he would not have to enter the encampment of the sick, and said, "I will go," motioning to the herd, "when you hear me shoot, you will know I have taken a buffalo. Then you and the others may come and help with the butchering."

"Yes, yes, we will," declared Carries and turned to run to the encampment to tell the others. Gabe watched her leave, looked down at Wolf and said, "All right boy, we're gonna have some buffalo steak tonight!"

***

He hugged the river until they came to a dry run-off creek bed that came from the far edge of the flats and bent around behind the grazing herd. With Wolf at his side, he moved up the gulley to work his way closer to the buffalo. As he moved, he heard the low rumble of so many of the bison, a gurgling bellow that sounded as if they were talking to one another or mumbling to themselves. The grass was thick and deep, giving the impression the brown monsters were moving without legs, their beards dragging on the green. Gabe lifted up over the edge of the coulee, spotted some cows together and no calves nearby, and worked a little closer.

The biggest beast of the plains had few predators, at least here in the flats, but nearer the mountains the timber wolves would attack as a pack and take down a buffalo, and the grizzly could take one down, but neither of those predators prowled the plains and the bison showed no concern. When Gabe was situated, he picked out two cows, and if he had additional shots, there was another cow and a couple young bulls. He lay the powder horn beside his perch, his possibles bag nearby, and lay five balls atop the bag. He stretched out the Ferguson, brought the hammer to full cock, moved his finger from the back trigger to the front, and lined up the front blade with the rear buckhorn sight. He took a deep breath, let some out, and slowly squeezed the front trigger.

The sudden roar from the Ferguson split the quiet of the flats, making some of the nearby buffalo twitch, but few moved a step. The targeted cow dropped where she stood, the big slug taking her just behind the front leg and burrowing deep into her chest to strike her heart, killing her instantly. Gabe quickly brought the rifle back, spun the trigger guard to open the breech, stuffed the patched ball into the breech, filled it with powder, and spun the guard back to close the breech and cut off the excess powder. He had flipped up the frizzen and put the powder in the pan, slapped the frizzen down and brought the Ferguson to his shoulder. Within moments, he had dropped four buffalo, three cows and a young bull, and the herd had started moving away. The beasts weren't frightened, just concerned. There was no stampede, but they moved quickly away, and were soon out of range, but still in sight. They slowed, and began grazing again, no longer concerned about the disturbance.

Gabe started to the carcasses, saw the women and the two boys already coming toward him, leading three horses, and talking animatedly, as they waved at Gabe. He lifted his hand in a wave, and went to the downed animals, checking each one to be certain they were dead. He knew that among the plains tribes, the work of butchering was the work of the women, but he offered to help and was put to work skinning. The two youngsters were fascinated by the big wolf, but Gabe cautioned them to keep their distance. Normally, Wolf was friendly, but when fresh meat was involved, he was too focused on his meal to be friendly.

Wasting little time, the women had a fire going and strip steaks simmering, and Gabe noticed a pair of smoke racks that were already decorated with thin strips of lean meat soaking up the alder smoke that rose from the hot coals beneath. When Carries saw him looking at the racks, she said, "That is for you. We will smoke our meat later, but that is for you."

Gabe grinned, "I am grateful. I seldom have time to smoke any meat. I will definitely enjoy it!" He grinned as he returned to the skinning of the bull, the last of the carcasses to shed their hides. They worked well into the night and the carrion eaters had already begun picking over the waste piles, turkey vultures, ravens, coyotes, a badger, and an eagle, all jostled about for their fair share, but several times, Wolf sent them all scattering, just because he could.

As they worked, they talked, and Gabe learned much about the Assiniboine. One of the women was fluent in Spanish and English, and made the conversation multi-lingual, with the Siouan dialect of the Assiniboine language, French, Spanish, and English all jumbled and with a little sign language to clarify, they learned about one another.

Gabe learned they referred to themselves as *Hohe Nakota* and that they were once a part of the Sioux people. They were also called Stone Sioux, because they cooked with heated stones dropped into pots of water to cook their food. Their band was so called by the French and meant *Big Devils* because they were such good traders and warriors and horse thieves. The women chuckled when Carries said they were thieves, and she clarified as she pointed to the horses, "Those were stolen from the Crow to the south." Gabe chuckled, but remembered his friends among the Crow and their animosity toward the Blackfoot and the Assiniboine.

As women are wont to do everywhere, the older and somewhat portly one of the three asked Gabe, "Do you have a woman? Or do you just have a wolf for a friend?"

Gabe chuckled, "I had a woman. She was killed by a Bannock. I killed him." Although he knew he had not struck the death blow, he also knew he was responsible for the man's death and didn't care to tell the whole story. He sucked in another deep breath that lifted his shoulders, choked on it as he stifled a sob, for he realized the old woman, known as Make Cloud Woman, was inquiring for a reason.

"Do you not have a man?" asked Gabe, trying to remain as stoic as possible.

The women giggled together, but the old woman said, "I have had two men and now I am on man number three!" she declared, slapping her leg as she laughed. "I am too much woman for one man!"

The others laughed, and Gabe turned to them, speaking to the French speaking one known as Two Crows, "And what about you two? Do you have a man?"

Gabe grinned as he watched Two Crows, a woman of about forty summers and showing her years, duck her head and say, "I have a good man, but he is sick now." Then she lifted her head, smiled, and nodded toward Carries and said, "But she does not have a man!"

Carries threw a scrap of meat at the woman, acting perturbed with her telling and busied herself with the remaining meat.

"So, surely a woman like you has a lot of men looking to you for their woman?" asked Gabe.

She lifted her head proudly, "There have been men that want to make me their woman, but I have not found one that is suitable."

Gabe lifted his eyebrows, nodded his head slowly, and added, "Then I'm sure the right one will come for you soon." She gave him a sidelong glance and focused on her work, ending the conversation with, "We must get this done. It will soon be light, and the sick will be hungry."

***

Gabe made his camp near where he pulled the canoe ashore and rolled out his blankets to catch a little sleep before first light. He was tired but satisfied with the kills and helping the people nearby. He had asked about the sick, concerned it might be smallpox that had taken its toll among many of the native people, and was relieved to find it was a mild form of cholera or something similar based on the symptoms. They said the sick were improving and should be up and around within a day or two.

He was loading the canoe and getting ready to leave when he heard a hail from behind and turned to see Carries Her Kettle approaching with a sizable parfleche. She smiled as she neared, offered the parfleche to Gabe, "That is the smoked meat for you. I made some pemmican also. It is to thank you for the buffalo."

Gabe grinned as he accepted the parcel, "I thank you for this. I will enjoy this for many days as I travel, and I will think of you each time."

Carries dropped her eyes, then lifted up to look at Gabe. "Because you came, we can feed those who are sick. They will grow strong and get well. You are a friend to the *Wadópahna Tuwa.*"

Gabe turned to add the new parfleche to his gear, motioned Wolf into the canoe, and looked back to Carries, wondering if every woman he would see would be compared to Otter. He nodded, stepped into the canoe and pushed off, lifting his paddle to wave to the woman who stood watching as the current carried him away. As he thought of those he met and helped, he chuckled as he considered the name of the band and how it meant Big Devils, *So, I made a deal with the devils!* and dipped his paddle deep for a long reach and moved into the river, anxious to make good time. He had a long way to go.

9 / Traders

For two weeks he rode the water of the Missouri, its twisting, winding course taking him across prairie lands, rolling hills, and alongside high rising rocky faced hillsides. He pushed past the confluence of the Yellowstone that carried its muddy waters into the green of the Missouri, coloring it all a murky brown. And into the third week, the waters slowly turned to the south and Gabe knew they were leaving the land of the Assiniboine and nearing the territory of the Hidatsa and Mandan.

Mid-day, after the river had turned due south, Gabe spotted what he guessed to be a trader's cabin. The river had widened and a long spit of sand split the water with the majority of the current's flow bearing to his right and a confluence with another river pushed the craft closer to the sandy bar, but Gabe back paddled and side-slipped to the low bank away from the cabin. Once aground, he looked toward the log structure, saw a corral with a few horses, several pirogues pulled to ground behind the cabin, and a handful of horses and natives standing out front.

Gabe slipped the rifle from the scabbard, cradled the Ferguson in the crook of his left arm and motioned to Wolf to heel beside him. He walked slowly to the cabin, keeping a watchful eye on both the natives and the surrounding terrain for any others that might approach. As he neared, two natives came from the cabin, followed by a white man, obviously the trader. As the natives mounted up, the trader caught sight of Gabe and he turned to look. With a frown wrinkling his forehead, the man stood with one thumb under his galluses, the other hand holding a clay pipe at his mouth. His rumpled hair covered his ears and collar, his buckskin britches were tucked into his tall lace-up boots, yet bright eyes peered from under heavy eyebrows. A slow grin painted the man's face and he lifted a hand to motion Gabe closer.

As Gabe neared, Wolf watched the natives depart, although they were gesticulating and talking about the man with the big wolf, and Gabe kept Wolf close beside him. The trader greeted Gabe, "Well, if you are not a sight for sore eyes! And where might you be coming from?" he asked, the wide grin showing tobacco stained teeth.

"Upriver. On my way downriver," answered Gabe, noncommittally. He stepped closer, held out his hand to shake, "I'm Gabe, Gabe Stone."

"Good to meet you, Gabe Stone. I am René Jusseaume, and this here's my tradin' post. Need some
supplies do ye?"

"Oh, maybe some coffee, powder, and sugar. Not
much."

"Well, come on in, and we'll get you outfitted. Got
some pelts do you?" asked Jusseaume, speaking over
his shoulder as he turned into the cabin.

The interior was dim with one window and the
door letting in the only light, although a pair of candles
smoked at the edge of a plank that served as a counter.
Shelves lined the side walls and part of the back wall,
most of the goods displayed were the usual trade goods
sought by the natives, beads, needles, copper pots, trade
fusils, vermillion and more. A quick glance told Gabe
the shelves were lacking in goods, but bundles of pelts
told of a good trading season.

"No pelts, gold coin do?" asked Gabe, stepping to
the counter.

The trader turned with a frown, "Gold coin? I haven't seen gold coin since two winters past when we
were stocking up for this trip. Where'd you say you
were coming from?"

"Upriver. Done some tradin' with Alexander Henry and the Northwest Company."

"How far upriver?" asked the overly curious Jusseaume. It was not the custom to be too curious about another
man's affairs and most considered it downright rude, but

Gabe knew the traders were always competing for the native trade and would naturally be concerned about what the other trading companies were accomplishing.

"The headwaters of the Missouri," answered Gabe, lifting the bag of coffee to examine.

"The headwaters? I thought this post was the furthest north of all posts," answered the trader, somewhat confused and disconcerted. "Surely, they haven't established a post there, have they?"

Gabe grinned, "No, they just had a wall tent and were doin' some tradin', but they were more concerned with finding a passage to the Pacific. They were leavin' same time I left."

The trader sighed heavily, his concern relieved, and he looked at Gabe, "So, you've been to the headwaters, eh? How'd you get there?"

"Overland. Came from the south along the Rockies."

"And how'd you get here?"

"Downriver, got a canoe down yonder."

"And you're goin' downriver, St. Louis?"

"Ummhmm."

The trader was in thought as he gathered the rest of the goods for Gabe, paused at the counter, knocking the dottle from his pipe. He repacked it, lit it, blew a cloud of smoke to the side, then with a conspiratorial expression on his face, leaned on the counter and looked at Gabe. "So, could you guide an expedition to the headwaters?"

Gabe stood sideways to the counter, leaning his

hip against it and looked at the trader, "Just what are you thinkin'?"

"This tradin' business is gettin' more cutthroat than ever. What with Northwest and Hudson's moving in on everybody, makes it hard to make a profit. I've been talkin' with others, Jacques Clamorgan, Régis Loisel, and others, and everyone thinks the one that makes it furthest up the Missouri can capture the trade with several tribes and make a very good profit. But, no one knows anyone that's been there, till now."

"Well, I'm bound for St. Louis, after that, come spring, I'll be goin' back to the mountains, but I don't know for sure just how I'll be goin'. I'm not so sure I wanna travel with a bunch of pilgrims and traders."

"Well, if you don't want to be accosted by every trader in the business and many others that want to be, if'n I were you, I'd not let 'em know that you've been up the river," declared the trader, standing and taking a puff on the clay pipe.

Gabe gathered up his booty, handed a single coin to the trader, and waited for the man to make change. As Jusseaume looked at the coin, he looked at Gabe, "Got'ny more o' these?"

"That's the last one," answered Gabe. Although he still had an ample amount remaining from the heavy pouch of coins his father had given him, he was not about to let anyone know he had any more. The trader gave a slow nod, looking at Gabe, judging whether he was being truthful.

"So, how many traders are there along the river 'fore I get to St. Louis?"

The trader leaned on the counter, "Well, let's see. When we came up, the two traders I mentioned, Clamorgan and Loisel, they had a post about a week, ten days south, it was on the south end of an island. Then where the Niobrara joins the Missouri in the Ponca country, Solomon Petit was tryin' to make way, and at the Platte, Derouin was buildin' one. Past there at the Kansas river, Auguste and Pierre Choteau have a good post, and a little further, a couple fellas, Cabanné and Sarpy, were tryin' to get started. But for all I know, they could all be gone, or there could be several others. This business is not the safest thing to be doin', nosiree. Too many natives that don't like what you trade, and 'fore you know it you're standin' in the middle of a pile of ashes, hopin' you don't lose your hair!"

"I see what you mean. This is Mandan country, isn't it?" asked Gabe.

"It is. But we also get some Hidatsa and Arikara, and the other day I had some Teton Sioux come in, scared the daylights out of me, cuz they don't get along with the others, but it went well, no fighting and made some good trades." He paused, then asked, "What tribes did you meet up with further north?"

Gabe grinned, "Well, I hunted with the Assiniboine, hid from the Gros Ventre, ate with the Blackfoot, fought some too, camped with the Shoshone and

Bannock, fought beside the Crow. But there's also the Kootenai, Salish, Nez Perce, Arapaho, and more."

The trader shook his head in wonder, "And you've been among all those and still have your hair. That's a wonder."

"Ahh, most of 'em are good people. Not much different than you an' me and all the others, no matter what language they talk or how they wear their hair or how they dress, they're just people." He looked at the trader, grinned, picked up his bundle and turned to leave. Wolf had lain beside the door and rose when Gabe exited. The trader looked at the big beast, then to the man, and back at the wolf, "That there's a mighty big wolf. Ain't never seen one that big before."

"He's my friend and companion. Been with me since he was a pup, few days old." Gabe reached down to run his fingers through Wolf's scruff, then started toward the water. He turned to lift a hand in farewell to the trader, then walked to the canoe. With a glance to the clear sky, he knew there were several hours of travel time left in this day, and he was anxious to put some water behind him.

10 / Changes

The moon was waxing full and Gabe chose to use the night to make progress. Just over a week past his stop at the trader Jusseaume, he passed the remains of a post on the south end of a long island. Three more weeks brought him to the confluence of the Niobrara and the Missouri to see the remains of another post. He pushed on to the confluence of the Platte, but it was in the wee hours of the morning and he passed the small post Jusseaume told about that Solomon Petit was struggling with, and there didn't appear to be any signs of life around the deteriorating structure.

Ten more nights on the water and he pushed into the early light of day as he came to the confluence of the Kansas and Missouri rivers where sat a stone building with two out buildings and two corrals. Gabe grinned, recognizing this structure as one similar to another trading post of Choteau that he had visited when he stayed with the Osage. The Missouri made a broad bend to the east and the Kansas River pushed in from the west. Gabe navigated the canoe into the brushy bank at the point of land of the confluence. The post sat back at the edge of the thicket of trees on the point and Gabe held the craft's prow to the bank as he motioned Wolf out, then he stepped into the shallows to pull the craft ashore. He slipped the canoe under the overhang of the willows, then with rifle in hand, started for the post.

He noticed familiar trees that he hadn't seen since leaving Pennsylvania, hickory, elm, tulip, oak and more. He smelled some honeysuckle, saw the white blossoms and grinned at the memories made with Ezra as they romped through the woods, identifying all the trees, shrubs, and flowers on their journeys. Although it was early, first light was showing across the river and the morning sun was beginning to bounce lances of gold off the ripples of the river. As he stepped from the trees, he was hailed by a man standing in the doorway, startling another who was splitting some firewood for cooking. Both men stood and looked at Gabe as he approached. The man in the doorway was familiar, and Gabe grinned as he recognized Auguste Choteau.

Gabe grinned as he approached, hand extended to shake, "Mr. Choteau, it is good to see you again!"

The confused look on Auguste's face wrinkled his brow, but he extended his hand as he looked closer at the young man before him. Gabe saw the expression and as he shook the man's hand, "I'm sure you don't remember me, I was clean shaven then and a couple years younger. We met at your Fort Carondelet in Osage country. It was shortly after you built it and you were just getting the one on the Verdigris underway."

Choteau let a smile cross his face, "Yes, yes. But if I remember correctly, you were traveling with a colored man and a woman of the Osage, am I right?"

Gabe grinned, "Yes, you are. My friend, Ezra, stayed with the Shoshone and I am on my way to St. Louis to tend to some business. Thought I might stop off and have a cup of coffee, if you have any to spare!"

"Certainly, certainly. Come right in, the coffee should be ready and we're happy to share."

As the men were seated at the lone table that sat under a window and apart from the trade counter, Choteau asked, "So, you've been to the mountains, how exciting for you. The wilderness appears to agree with you, you've still got your hair and you look healthy enough. Did you get acquainted with many of the native peoples?"

Gabe grinned, "Since that's about all there is out there, yes we did. However, we did have a run-in or two with some of the less scrupulous French traders and others. But, that's the way of the territory."

"And were there any traders?"

"A few. We did meet Alexander Henry and David Thompson of the Northwest Company, but other than that, just a couple traders upstream on the Missouri."

"And were the natives friendly?"

"Most were, but they have their own ways and enemies, as to be expected." Gabe paused, sipped the steaming coffee, savoring the freshness, and looked to Choteau, "You seem to be prospering here."

"Not for long."

"Oh?"

"Yes. As you know, this is Spanish territory and subject to the rule of the appointed Governor General. We've had good relations, mostly, until the new man, Manuel Maria de Salcedo. He favors the Spanish traders and wants to turn all trade with the natives over to them. We'll be closing this post and moving everything to St. Louis," he mused as he looked around the interior of the post.

"I'm sure that's not going to be the end of your trading ventures, is it?"

"Oh no! Of course not. We have our business in St. Louis, and we'll be adding to our trading house and expanding our fur trading business. I really feel there will be a considerable increase in the fur trade in the coming years. And with the election coming, I think Jefferson will do well and I like some of his ideas regarding the territories."

Gabe sat back, enjoying his coffee, considering what Choteau said and asked, "All pelts, or just beaver?"

"Oh all pelts, of course. But, beaver will be in great demand. There seems to be a rising demand in Europe for the beaver. Seems they make great felt from the pelts."

Gabe pursed his lips as he nodded his head. "Well, I'm going to be in St. Louis for the winter, won't be returning to the mountains till spring, so, maybe we'll see each other in town." He stood, lifted his rifle to his arm, and extended his hand to shake with the trader.

Choteau stood, "By all means, when you are in St. Louis, don't hesitate to look me up. I have a home on the west side, and you will be welcome."

The men shook hands and Gabe stepped from the post, paused for a look around, and turned back to Choteau, "Thank you for the coffee, and I will certainly look you up when we're in St. Louis. I'm not sure where I'll be staying, but it probably won't be in town. I've grown accustomed to looking at the stars while I fall asleep and can't do that when there's a roof overhead."

Choteau grinned, nodding his head, and waved to Gabe as he walked toward the river. Wolf came from the trees, startling Choteau, but when Gabe reached down to stroke his head, the trader grinned, shook his head and turned back to the post.

Although he had traveled through the night, Gabe pushed back into the river and soon put the post well behind him. By mid-morning he was ready for some shut eye and when he spotted a likely camp, he put the craft on shore. With little wasted effort, Gabe and Wolf were soon stretched out on a bed of leaves under the long branches of a massive oak and were enjoying a time of rest.

It was a long ten days. He passed a pair of keel boats, and few pirogues, and one dugout. Each time he took cover, having been warned about some of the river pirates that rode the Missouri. With settlements springing up along the river, there were more targets for the rogues and river travel was becoming danger-ous, especially for those alone like Gabe. But he was well experienced and with Wolf as his lookout, the ten days were uneventful.

Early on day eleven from the post of Choteau, he began seeing farms near the river, and by mid-day, the first settlement stood at river's edge on the north bank. He knew this was not St. Louis, as Choteau had told him the town of his trading house was on the south bank of the Missouri, but more on the west bank of the Mississippi. He pushed on and in a short while, was surprised to see a ferry making its way across the river to the north bank. He pointed the canoe to shore by the ferry landing and stepped out to be greeted by an old woman, sitting on a woven cane rocking chair and smoking a corn-cob pipe.

"Howdy!" came the greeting from a mostly tooth-less mouth. The wrinkled countenance was decorated with thin wisps of white hair that trailed from under a floppy felt hat.

Gabe returned the greeting, "Howdy! Mind if I pull my canoe up here?"

"He'p yo'self!"

When he had pulled the canoe clear of the water, he cradled his rifle and with Wolf at his side, he walked up the bank to where the woman was waiting. "That's a mighty big dog, you got there!" she declared as she looked at Wolf.

Gabe chuckled, "He's a wolf and this is his first time in civilization!"

"Ya don't say! What'chu doin' wit' a wolf?"

"Oh, we just kinda took to one another when he was a pup. Been together ever' since."

The woman scowled as she looked at Wolf, but Wolf just sat down beside Gabe's leg and looked back at her, tongue lolling.

"He ain't hungry, is he?" she asked.

Gabe chuckled, "He's always hungry. Just his nature, but he's good at getting his own food. By the way, what do they call this place?"

"The official name is *Marais des Liards.* That's what them Frenchies call it. But we'uns that have been here a spell call it Cottonwood Swamp." She puffed on her pipe, then cocked her head and looked at Gabe, "So, what brings you into our neck of the woods?"

"Headin' to St. Louis, but I'm needful of finding a horse. I'm thinkin' it might be hard to get around the town with my canoe, there."

The old lady grinned, "You're right about that." She dropped her gaze, thought a moment, then lifted her eyes to Gabe, "I reckon 'bout the best you're gonna do is to go to the Haines farm. They got a good bunch o' horses and mules, sell some ever now n' then."

"Sounds like what I need. How would I find the Haines farm?"

She twisted around in her chair, used the stem of her pipe to point, "Take that road yonder 'bout two miles. It's on the west side the road, big stone house."

"Would you have some place I could leave my things for a day or so?" asked Gabe, looking around.

"Ummhmm. That shed back yonder, next to the chicken coop. It'll be safe thar."

Gabe grinned, "I thank you ma'am." He went to the canoe and put the parfleche rig on Wolf, then picked up the saddle and started to the shed.

The woman looked at Wolf, grinned, "As big as he is, you oughta just put your saddle on him!"

"I would, but he might protest a little too much and I don't win too many arguments with him."

They were soon finished stowing their gear, even to putting the canoe behind the shed, and were on their way to the Haines farm, hopeful of getting a horse to make it into town.

11 / Crowds

The two friends, Gabe and Wolf, walked side by side down the roadway that was lined on both sides with the many hardwoods standing tall and spreading their leafy branches to arch across the road, making the route appear as a leafy tunnel. Thick underbrush grew wherever sunlight pierced the canopy of green, and it was a pleasant walk. The shade offered a coolness unknown on the sun-splashed river, and the sounds of the forest were like a symphony to the ears of Gabe, sounds that tugged at his heartstrings to bring forth memories of a childhood long ago.

A fox squirrel scolded the passersby from a high branch on a massive oak, while across the road and high up in a dark elm, an opossum peered around the trunk to see what was disturbing the quiet. A break in the cover showed trees near the water with one holding the nest of a pair of osprey feeding their young, while a hawk circled overhead. Gabe couldn't help grinning as he enjoyed the stroll in the woods.

The two miles or so became more like four miles and the roadway opened into a broad area of fields and farms. On the right or west side of the roadway, a stone and rail fence bordered the road, petitioning off a wide meadow with several horses and mules grazing. Gabe stopped and leaned on the top rail, looking at the horses, then a glance to his left showed a steep-roofed stone house with a surrounding veranda and a pair of dormers on the front that stood above the veranda porch. A sizeable barn with a pair of corrals, and tack shop, and other sheds sat behind the house. The entire property was well kept and tended, and the house was inviting. Gabe turned from the fence, looked to Wolf, "Well boy, let's see if they are interested in selling a horse, shall we?"

The roadway to the house split the rail fence, but with a gate that hung between two tall posts with a cross beam and a sign hanging underneath that said simply, 'Haines'. Gabe grinned, turned from the main road and started up the roadway to the house. He pushed open the gate, swung it back and latched it, then walked between the pole and stone fences to the house. As he neared, he saw someone sitting in a rocking chair on the veranda and watching him approach. Gabe called out, "Hello the house! Mind if I come in?"

From the shadows stepped a woman, wavy brown

hair falling to her shoulders over a high-waisted button up dress that covered her ankles. It was a muted green pattern, with long sleeves but did little to hide her womanly features. As she stepped into the light, Gabe guessed her to be about twenty, and quite attractive. She lifted one hand to a porch post as she leaned slightly toward it and answered, "Yes, you may come close."

She watched as Gabe and Wolf drew near, and at the sight of Wolf, she stepped back slightly, as she stared at the big canine. She looked at Gabe, saw a somewhat scruffy, bearded, and probably dirty man with broad shoulders, deep chest, and a confident stride. It was difficult to judge his age or see much of his face what with the floppy felt hat that covered his brow. But his voice was clear and deep, and his manner was pleasant and non-threatening.

Gabe touched the brim of his hat, gave a slight nod, "Afternoon ma'am, or is it miss?"

"It's Miss, Miss Elizabeth Haines, and you are?"

"Oh, excuse me, I didn't expect to see such a charming image. You're the first white woman I've seen in years! Oh, my name is Gabe, Gabe Stone, and I'm lookin' to buy a horse, if you have any you would consider selling. Or is there someone else I should speak to?"

Elizabeth paused, leaning her head to the side as she looked this man over, then answered, "We might have a horse or two to sell. Forgive me for asking, but do you have the wherewithal to pay for a horse, Mr. Stone?"

Gabe grinned, "Well now, I guess that all depends on what kind of a price you might have on your horses, Miss Haines. But, yes, I have the means to purchase a horse."

"Then let's take a look at a few, but first, let me get a bonnet." Without waiting for a response, she turned away and disappeared into the house, but within a few moments, returned with both a thin shawl over her shoulders and a flat brimmed, low crowned hat that shaded her eyes. She descended the four steps to ground level and walked toward Gabe, motioning for him to follow as she led the way to one of the corrals beside the barn.

As they walked, Gabe asked, "So, is this your farm, Miss Haines?"

"It is my brother's and mine. Our father established the farm, built the house, but went off to fight in the war and never returned. I was an infant, my brother four years older, and my mother never remarried and passed just a year ago. My brother and I have managed the farm since her death."

"It's a beautiful place, you've done well."

She glanced up at Gabe, turned to the corral and went to the fence. She pointed to the animals, "Any of these are for sale, except the dapple grey, she's mine."

Gabe stood his rifle at the fence, stepped up to swing a leg over the top rail, and sat looking at the horses. There was an assortment of eight horses, all good-looking animals, quarter-horses, standard bred, and thoroughbred, but almost immediately, a spirited buckskin quarter horse caught his eye. It stood just over fifteen hands, long backed, broad rump, well-muscled chest, and a slight arch to his neck that told of her spirited nature as she confidently tossed her head. With black legs, mane and tail, and a jagged blaze of black on her face, Gabe was immediately smitten. He slid from the rail, stood quiet, then slowly stretched out his hand and began to speak softly. He looked directly at the buckskin, ignoring the others, and the horse looked back at him. The mare tossed her head and took a step toward Gabe. Then as both stood still, Gabe spoke softly, and the buckskin started toward him. With just a few steps, she stood before Gabe, stretched out her nose and accepted Gabe's touch like they were old friends. Gabe stepped closer, put a hand to the side of the mare's neck, ran his fingers through her mane, and stepped beside him to drape his arm over her withers.

Gabe grinned, looked up at Elizabeth, "This one." He walked toward the fence and the buckskin followed closely behind.

The woman looked at Gabe, then to the horse, and said, "Now that's surprising, she's not been too friendly before, and I thought you'd choose a stallion or a gelding."

Gabe grinned, "Usually I would, but," nodding to the mare, "we understand each other."

Wolf had stayed by the fence near the woman and stood as Gabe came near. The buckskin spotted him and stepped forward, stretching her nose to the space between the poles and Wolf did the same. The two touched noses, and looked at each other, somehow knowing they would be friends. Gabe climbed over the fence to drop down between Wolf and Elizabeth.

She asked, "I was just getting ready to have some tea. Would you care to join me?"

Gabe grinned, "I would be delighted, if you think you can stand this scruffy appearance of mine. I haven't had a chance to clean up since I arrived."

As they stepped up on the veranda, Elizabeth motioned him to be seated at the table and she went to the door. "Sophie! Could you bring us some tea, please?"

Gabe heard a response, "Yes'm" come from within the house as he seated himself.

Elizabeth joined him and as he stood, she seated herself. Gabe sat just as she asked, "So, how is it that you haven't seen a white woman in years?"

Gabe grinned, "I've been in the mountains for the past, oh, 'bout five years."

"The mountains? What mountains?"

"The Rocky Mountains, out west a ways."

"My, I thought that was wilderness with nothing but Indians!"

Gabe grinned, and let her draw her own conclusions, which she did as she answered, "Oh, I see. So, what brings you to St. Louis? Did you bring in some furs like the other wild men in buckskins?"

Again Gabe chuckled, "No ma'am, I have some business to attend to, then I plan on returning to the west. But, probably not till spring. Which brings to mind, would you know of any boarding houses between here and St. Louis where a man could put up for the winter?"

Elizabeth cocked her head to the side and gave him a sidelong glance, then asked, "Do you plan to work for your board and room, Mr. Stone?"

"If I have to, but not till after I finish my business dealings," he answered, catching the look she was giving him as if she were measuring him for a task or something.

"My brother will be back later this evening. We have had occasional boarders and workers stay with us before and might use one again. However, I will have to discuss it with my brother. Now, about this horse you want . . ."

They dickered over tea, often laughing and enjoying the banter, but in the end, Gabe settled-up for the purchase of the buckskin and a strawberry roan that he would use as a pack horse. As they finished, he stood, counted out the coin to pay for the horses, halters and bridles and packs, then turned to leave. "If I may, I would like to stop back by after I get my gear and meet your brother."

"I'm sure that would be fine, Mr. Stone."

Gabe grinned, "Gabe, please, just Gabe."

She smiled, "And you may call me Miss Haines," and nodded slightly, showing a touch of mischievousness in her eyes. Then she added, "Or if you prefer, you may call me Elizabeth."

Gabe touched the brim of his hat, smiled and stepped from the veranda to go to the corrals for the horses. Within moments, he had the bridle and halter on the pair, grabbed a handful of mane and swung aboard to ride bareback for the return to the ferry landing and his gear.

12 / Friends

Dusk was settling in over the farmland as Gabe rode up to the gate of the Haines farm. He bent down to lift the latch, pushed the gate open, went through and turned back to re-latch. As he sat up, he twisted around to look to the veranda and seeing no one, rode closer to the house. He called out, "Hello the house!" and waited. Elizabeth pushed open the door, followed by a man that almost mirrored her image. Tall, ramrod straight, dark hair and clean-shaven, a broad smile split his face as he stepped from behind his sister. He held the hand of another woman, obviously his wife, and he lifted his free hand in a greeting. "Welcome! You must be the Mr. Stone my sister was telling me about. Step down." He grinned as he watched Gabe rein up and sit his saddle.

"That's right. At least the last time I checked, that's who I was. And you must be Rupert Haines. And is that fine lady your wife?" asked Gabe as he swung his leg over the rump of the buckskin to step down.

"She is." He looked to his wife and back to Gabe, "This is Eloise." The woman smiled, gave a slight curtsy, and stood beside Elizabeth.

"Pleased to meet you, ma'am," responded Gabe, touching the brim of his hat, holding the rein of the buckskin in his free hand. He looked to Elizabeth, "And to see you again, Miss Haines," added Gabe, nodding toward the sister.

She smiled and nodded, "I spoke to my brother about having you stay on, and he's quite agreeable." She nodded toward her brother and before Gabe could respond he added, "That's right. I could always use some help around the place from time to time. We have a small cabin, shed really, out back that used to serve as servant's quarters, but our help has their own room in the main house. If that would suit, you're welcome to use it as long as you like."

"I'm sure it will be fine, although I'm kind of out of the habit of sleeping under a roof, but I'm sure I can become accustomed." He turned to mount up to go to his new quarters but was stopped by the uplifted hand of Rupert.

"After you put your things away and put the horses in the corral, come back and we'll have coffee on the veranda and talk a spell," suggested Rupert with a smile.

Gabe nodded as he reined the buckskin around, "I'll do that. Thank you."

***

It was a short while until Gabe returned, and the three were seated around the small table on the veranda, and they waved him up to join them. "Have a seat, have a seat," offered Rupert, waving him to the remaining chair. He no sooner was seated than a matronly looking colored woman, her girth covered by a frilled apron, sat a plate with a very large slice of chocolate cake before him and one before each of the others. She stepped around Wolf, who lay beside Gabe, and poured fresh coffee from a silver urn into the four cups seated on saucers at each place, stepped back and asked, "Any'thin' else, ma'am?" as she looked to Eloise.

Eloise smiled, "No, that will be all, thank you Sophie." The woman nodded, turned away and disappeared into the house.

Gabe watched her go and asked, "Slave?"

Elizabeth answered, "Oh no! Sophie and her husband Jonathan, are free. They were given their manumission papers by my mother, who was a staunch anti-slavery advocate." She frowned and looked at Gabe, "And where do you stand on the issue of slavery, *Mr.* Stone?"

Gabe grinned, knowing it was a loaded question and took a sip of coffee before answering. "Well, let me answer you in this way, *Miss* Haines. My best friend, who is more of a brother than friend, and I grew up together, doing everything together and even sharing dreams. His name is Ezra, and when it became necessary for me to leave Philadelphia, he refused to let me go alone and we left to fulfill our dreams in the mountains. We even married sisters," his eyes dropped and showed a pensive reflection for a moment, then he lifted his head to continue, but before he could, Elizabeth interjected, "I don't see what that has to do with the slavery issue."

Gabe grinned, "Ezra's father is the senior pastor of the Mother Bethel African Episcopal Church in Philadelphia, the largest congregation of coloreds in the state. You see, Elizabeth, my best friend and brother is what you would call a free colored," and Gabe chuckled, then added, "Although he sometimes refers to himself as Black Irish!"

"But that still doesn't explain . . ." she began again, but Gabe stayed her question with an uplifted hand.

"In our travels, we have encountered slave catchers whose practice is to take any colored and free or not, turn him in as a runaway slave. They also take Indians and sell them into slavery. And at every turn, we have fought them, freed their captives, and ended their dastardly practices. So, you see, *Miss* Haines, I not only disagree with the practice of slavery, I fight against it."

She looked at him through slightly squinted eyes, relaxed, smiled and sat back, "I see. And, I thought we had agreed to use first names, did we not? The way you hiss *Miss* makes me cringe." She looked at him with a smile as she sipped her coffee, watching him over the rim of the cup.

"Yes, we did, Elizabeth. Peace?" he questioned, looking at her as he stabbed at the cake with the fork.

She smiled, and nodded, "Of course, Gabe." She looked at the cake and added, "Enjoy your cake. I think you'll find it delectable."

Rupert and Eloise had watched the interchange between the two, Eloise smiling all the while, until Rupert spoke up, "So, you've come all the way from the Rocky Mountains to conduct a little business here in St. Louis, may I be of assistance in any way?"

Gabe looked to Rupert and leaned back in the chair, "Well, I reckon I can find my way around the town alright, but I would like you to tell me all about the big city. Just how big is St. Louis?"

Rupert chuckled, "Well, it's no Philadelphia, but it is a growing town. Last I heard there's about eighteen hundred within the close proximity of the city, but closer to twenty-five hundred round about."

Gabe grinned, "When I left Philadelphia, there were over forty thousand there, most said it was the largest city in the states."

Rupert twisted a little in his chair, getting comfortable as he leaned his elbows on the table, looking directly at Gabe. "It's got a long way to go to get that many, and I hope it never does. Too many folks now, most of 'em speakin' French, and the rest a conglomeration of languages, but business gets done. I make as few trips into the city as necessary, just for supplies, mostly. But there's just about anything you might need. Course the biggest is the Trading House of Choteau, but there are others, you know, gunsmiths, merchants, tradesmen, and even a doctor. I heard tell of a lawyer settin' up shop, and, oh yeah, the bank's expanding. There's a boat builder, and a wheelwright that's makin' some wagons and turned out a mighty fine carriage for the Choteau's. There's the beginnings of a hotel, three eating places, and plenty of taverns. Seems the Coureur des Bois that come in from the north with their pelts, trade 'em, and whatever they get they spend, usually on supplies, but plenty of them drink it up and then have to find work to make enough for another trip after furs."

He reached out, moving the cups and saucers aside and dipped his finger in the coffee in the saucer and began to draw on the table top, "Now, all along the river here and parallel to the water, they've built a stone wall, and then there's a row of buildings, broken up into blocks." He paused, looked to Gabe, "The French laid it out in a grid," and began to draw again. "This first street is what some of us are calling First Street and so on, but the real name is *La Rue de la Place,* Second Street, *La Rue d'Eglise,* and Third Street, *La Rue des Granges.*" He looked up again, dipped his finger in the liquid and continued, "Now these streets that run perpendicular to the river are Market Street, Walnut Street and Chestnut. Of course they have French names too, but most folks use the English. South of town on Mill Creek, there's a grist mill, just below Choteau's pond."

He paused for a bite of cake, accepted a refill of his coffee from Sophie, and continued, "Now, all this," he made a broad ranging motion to indicate the land that lay to the west of the city, "is what they call 'Commons'. Every land owner was given use of a strip about two hundred feet wide and about seventy-five hundred feet long, about three and a half acres, to use as he saw fit. Initially it was just used for gathering fire wood, putting stock on it and such, but then they started growin' crops on it and folks began to prosper a little. Not a bad idea, you think?"

"Sounds reasonable. Can folks sell it if they want?"

"The land? No, it's held by the Spanish and is for the growth of the city. But they can use it however they want. But that's why our father came to this place, he wanted his own land and nothing to do with the government. It was a smart decision."

Gabe looked to the field and around, "You have a mighty nice place here. Well-kept."

Rupert grinned, appreciating the compliment, "We have good crops of corn, beans, and tobacco. Raise horses, cattle, mules, and of course the chickens, and such. Keeps us busy, and that's why I can use some help."

"Well, if it's alright with you, I would like to get my business settled first, shouldn't take too long, and then I'll be ready to do whatever I can to help. I do appreciate the place to stay, it will be quite comfortable and convenient."

Elizabeth chipped in, "We expect you at our table for every meal, such has always been our arrangement with others that have helped out around the place."

Gabe grinned, looked at Sophie as she started cleaning off the table, "Well, if the rest of her cooking is as good as that cake, you won't have to ring the dinner bell very loud. That was mighty fine, Sophie, thank you."

Gabe rose, gave a slight bow to the ladies, "Ladies, thank you for a very fine evening. Rupert, thank you for the information on your fair city, and for the opportunity to stay." He extended his hand to shake, then added, "I'm going to turn in, I plan on an early visit to town to settle things and hope to return by evening. I shall try to be back for the evening meal, but don't hold it for me. Thanks again." He nodded and turned away, motioned for Wolf to come and quickly descended the steps and went around the corner of the house to go to his cabin.

It was a small room that held a small table, two chairs, a counter with shelves above. A bunk with a down mattress and ample covers. A chifforobe that had seen considerable wear, and a small stove. Gabe put away his things, stood the saddle in the corner, but took the pistols to the bed and spent some time cleaning all his weapons, reloading each one, and setting them aside. Wolf lay at his feet, snoozing. Gabe thought as he worked, for he always considered this a time for planning and thinking out problems. His plan was to go into town and check with the bank first, then find a postman to see if there was any mail for him. After those things, then he could plan out the rest of his time.

He finished his cleaning, tidied up the place and turned in for the night, yet he lay for some time staring at the ceiling, hands clasped behind his head, remembering the time with Pale Otter, then thought about Elizabeth. He grinned, rolled over and was soon asleep.

13 / Town

By first light, Gabe had spent his time with his Lord
out behind the little cabin on the banks of the small
creek that twisted through the farm. And seeing no
one up and about at the house, he saddled up and with
Wolf by his side started toward town. After the first
hour, Gabe reached down and stroked the buckskin's
neck, "Let's see what you can do, girl," and kicked him
up to a trot. The horse moved easily and smoothly,
her stride was long and gaited, and they covered a
lot of ground, then after about fifteen minutes, Gabe
pulled her back to a walk. It felt especially good to be
in the saddle again and have a good horse under him,
riding a canoe just isn't the same. The mare tossed her
head and Gabe knew the horse was raring to go and
after a couple miles of cooling off, he let her have her
head and kicked her up to a canter. Gabe was enjoying
the horse and the buckskin handled and responded

well, but Gabe slowed her to a walk, and chose to enjoy the rest of the ride and look over the scenery.

He had stripped the holsters and pistols from the saddle, left his bow and quiver of arrows behind, but the Ferguson rode in its familiar scabbard under his right leg, butt forward and easy to hand. His Bailes over/under was nestled in his belt that also held his tomahawk at his hip, and the familiar weight of the knives hung between his shoulder blades. Although he had washed up before leaving, he was looking forward to a bath and shave and haircut. Rupert had told him of a tonsorial parlor that catered to the well-to-do but wouldn't turn away anyone with the money to pay.

There were few people about when he rode into the town from the northwest, bypassing the commons and coming in on Third street. He passed several blocks that had portions fenced off with a house sitting behind. Most of the homes he saw were built of vertical logs set in the ground, chinked with sod and other unknown substances, all supporting a peaked roof. Most were about twenty by thirty feet with a stone chimney at one end. As he drew nearer the center of town there were more buildings and homes of stone construction, all with stone similar to the bluffs near the river. Some of the homes were sizable with porches or verandas, and a few had two stories.

He chose to ride through the town, look around and locate what he needed, then he would leave the horse and maybe Wolf at a livery. It took just a short while to ride the length of the town and back again, seeing most of the businesses and homes, several holding businesses as well as living quarters. He spotted a livery at the corner of Fourth and Olive, reined up at the big open double doors and called out between echoing rings of steel on steel that told of a blacksmith at work. A deep voice answered from within, "Yo! What'chu need?"

"Need to stable my horse for the day. Got'ny room?" asked Gabe of the darkness.

"Sho' do! Bring him on in!"

Gabe stepped down and with the rein in hand, led the buckskin into the dim interior. A shaft of early sunlight bent through the loft door and framed an anvil and big man in the light. The man stood about a hand taller than Gabe, a hand wider at the shoulders, and about two stone heavier. But his smile split his face and bright eyes showed from under his sweat slickened forehead as he wiped his face on his forearm and showed but few sprigs of hair across his dome. He looked at Gabe, "Mornin'! Stranger, ain'tcha?"

Gabe grinned, extended his hand, "Gabe's the name."

"I'm Bucky!" He motioned with the hammer in his left hand toward the stalls, "Take any one of 'em. There's grain in the barrel an' water out thar to the well. Should be a bucket in there, or you let him have a drink first, then put him away. I'd do it for ya, but gotta work this iron while it's hot and 'fore the weather gets too hot to stand around the forge."

"That's fine, and I thank you!" answered Gabe, leading the buckskin to the water trough. He noticed the big man look at Wolf as he walked past, then shake his head and return to his work. Gabe wasn't too sure how Wolf would react to so many people moving about, but he had done alright in the many Indian villages with lots of children and others that were busy with their lives and a little wary of the big wolf, but there had been nothing happen and Wolf had taken most things in stride. After putting up the buckskin, he asked the Blacksmith, "Think I need to carry my rifle with me, or should I leave it here?"

The big man grinned, "The only wild animals around here are the two-legged ones, and most of them won't give you time to get a rifle in the game. But I see you're carryin' a pistol and a hawk, prob'ly got a knife under there some'eres, so, I reckon you'll do alright with what'chur carryin'. But suit yourself, if'n you wanna leave it, it'll be safe with me. But if you're more comfortable with it in your arm, then go 'head on."

Gabe grinned, returned to his saddle and slipped the rifle into the scabbard, but hung the saddle bags over his shoulder. He nodded and grinned to Bucky as he walked out the door. His first stop was at a mercantile and bought a pair of woolen trousers, two linen drop shoulder shirts, a pair of boots, and the appropriate undergarments. With package in hand, he left the store, waving Wolf alongside. The wolf had stationed himself outside the door of the mercantile, but well back from the entry and lay alongside the stone wall, enjoying the coolness of the stone. The two walked side by side on the boardwalk as they made their way to the tonsorial parlor. Gabe stepped in, Wolf right behind him, and asked, "Do you gentlemen have baths?"

The nearest man had a pair of spectacles resting on the end of his nose and looked appraisingly at Gabe, and answered, "Two bits!"

Gabe flipped the man a coin and lifted his eyebrows to question the whereabouts, and the man motioned to the back. Yet when he saw the big wolf on the other side of the man, he stepped back and said, "Here, here! We can't have that beast in here!"

Gabe grinned, "You tell him," and kept walking, Wolf trailing close behind. As he exited the back door into a high fenced but small compound, two large half barrels loomed, and clear water showed. A colored man in short britches, a linen shirt, and high socks over buckle shoes, asked, "You gittin' a bath?"

"Ummhmm," answered Gabe, looking from one tub to the other.

The man motioned to the one nearest the far fence, "That'ns clean this mornin', you da fust!"

Gabe set his bundle on a bench and started removing his buckskins, and the attendant tossed him a big bar of lye soap, a brush, and a rag. Gabe grinned, lay them on the bench and finished undressing. He stepped into the cold water, looked at the attendant who grinned as he carried a bucket of hot water to the tub. Before Gabe sat down, the bucket of warm water made it more tolerable, and he began scrubbing. He enjoyed the bath, the first warm water since the hot springs in the Rockies, and he savored the experience. As he climbed out, the attendant handed him a big towel, and Gabe quickly dressed in his new duds.

As he walked into the parlor, he asked, "How 'bout a haircut and a shave?"

The bespectacled man that had been so critical before, grinned and waved a cape toward a chair and said, "I'll be happy to take care of you sir!"

Once the man was finished and held a mirror for Gabe to look, Gabe was surprised, but pleased with his look. Now with his dark blonde hair trimmed, his face clean-shaven, and new clothes, he was reminded of himself of years gone by and his time at university. He stood, paid the man, and slipped on his beaded buckskin jacket. Once outside, he slipped the pistol from the bundle, stuffed it in his belt, slipped in the tomahawk, and finally felt dressed. He grinned, waved to Wolf, put the saddlebags over his shoulder, the bundle under his arm, and started for the bank. He had spotted the Bank of North America on the corner of Second Street and Chestnut and knew that was the bank he needed, with the same name as the one in Philadelphia, he was certain they were connected.

Leaving Wolf outside to wait, he stepped into the bank, knowing he presented a rather unusual figure, what with his beaded buckskin jacket and saddle bags over his shoulder, but he let a broad smile split his face as he looked at the teller behind his barred cage and asked, "Is the manager available?"

Another appraising look was recognized by Gabe, but he leaned casually on the counter and added, "Would you tell him Mr. Gabriel Stonecroft is here to see him, please?"

The man lifted his head in a nod, raising one judgmental eyebrow and turned away without answering. He stepped to a door that had the name *Philip Dorman, Mgr.* in gold leaf on the frosted window, rapped his knuckles twice and hearing a voice from within, he opened the door and stepped in, closing the door behind him.

Gabe grinned, picturing what was happening inside and within a short moment, the door opened and a contrite teller came to the window, hands clasped before him as he bent slightly at the waist and said, "Mr. Dorman will see you now, *Mr.* Stonecroft!" and motioned to the half door at the end of the counter. He hastened to open the divider and motion Gabe to the door, opened it for him and closed it behind him.

Gabe stepped into the well-appointed office, extended his hand, "Mr. Dorman, Gabriel Stonecroft."

"Mr. Stonecroft! A pleasure to make your acquaintance, indeed. Please be seated." He motioned to the chair directly in front of his desk and as Gabe seated himself, the manager took his seat. "Well, sir. I was wondering just the other day if I would ever have the opportunity to meet you, and here you are! A pleasure indeed. So, how may I be of service?"

Gabe grinned, set his saddle bags and bundle beside him, leaned forward slightly and began, "First, I want to make certain that the transfer of my accounts was made successfully."

"I believe so, yessir. But, there is a matter of verification, for the safety of your accounts, you understand."

"Yes, I do, and just what do you need?"

He reached into the right-hand drawer of his desk, withdrew some papers, shuffled through them and said, "Oh, here we are." He read a little bit, then looked up at Gabe, "Mr. Sutterfield, the attorney for the estate lists three verification questions. First, your father's full name?"

"Boettcher Hamilton Stonecroft," answered Gabe.

"Your sister's married name?"

"Gwyneth Claiborne, married to Hamilton Claiborne."

"And the nephew of the Supreme Court justice, John Rutledge?"

Gabe frowned at this question as it had nothing

to do with his family or the estate, but he answered, "Jason Wilson."

The manager looked up at Gabe, smiled, and said, "Very good, very good. Thank you. Now, how may I help you."

"Mr. Sutterfield should have included a copy of the settlement of the estate with those papers, is that correct?"

"Yes, yes." He shuffled a few more papers, gathered a small stack, and handed it to Gabe.

"Good." He bent over to the saddlebags, extracted a draw-string pouch, and held it out to the manager, "I would also like a thousand dollars in gold coin from my account, if you would sir."

The man's eyes flared, he stuttered a moment, "Uh, certainly sir. I'm not certain we have that much gold coin on hand but let me check. Just a moment." He rose, bag in hand and left the office.

Gabe could hear the muffled conversation between the teller and the manager, dropped his head as he smiled slightly, and turned to see the manager step back in, bag in hand. "There you go, sir. Now, if you'll just sign this receipt . . ." and lay the paper before Gabe.

With a quick review of the figures, Gabe signed the receipt and looked to Dorman. He divided the coin between two pouches, placing one on either side of the saddle bags, and hung them over his shoulder as he prepared to stand. "I will leave the rest on deposit with you and if you need to contact me, I will be staying at the Haines farm northwest of town."

"Oh, certainly, sir. I know Rupert Haines, a fine gentleman and nice family."

Gabe stood, extended his hand to shake with the manager, nodded and said, "Thank you Mr. Dorman, a pleasure doing business with you. Oh, and I will be in touch with Mr. Sutterfield and my sister, there might be a need to transfer some funds back to your main bank in Philadelphia or to my sister in Washington. But, I will let you know if that becomes necessary."

"Certainly sir," he answered as he ushered Gabe to the door and bid him goodbye.

Gabe noticed the teller was missing, thought little of it and exited the building. But the hackles on his neck were raised as he looked back at the manager, who stood grinning in the doorway, but his expression didn't go any deeper than the sun on his face. There was something about the man that didn't set right with Gabe and he resolved to find out more about this manager of the bank, a man that should be above reproach, but the title on the door did little to reveal the depth of a man's character, nor his commitment or lack of same to moral integrity. There was something odd about the man, and the lingering thought about that question concerning Jason Wilson didn't sit well.

14 / Resolved

Under most circumstances, Gabe would be unconcerned about the bags of coin he carried. When he left
Philadelphia he had more than he now carried and
used less than half of the amount over the course of
five years of travel through the wilderness, with little
thought of robbery or loss. But now, the temperament
of the town was different, and his hackles kept him
on his guard. Wolf walked beside him, and he too
appeared wary. Gabe spoke to him, "Easy boy."

The bank was on the corner of Second and Chestnut, and he wanted to stop by the Trading Company
of Auguste Choteau that sat a couple of blocks away
at First and Market. If Auguste was there, he would
visit a spell, then return to the livery and start for
the cabin on the Haines farm. He glanced back to the
entry of the bank to see the teller come around the
corner and quickly duck inside, nothing casual about

his movement. Gabe took a deep breath, looked down the boardwalk past the different buildings on either side, saw a tall solid pole fence around a parcel of property between some buildings, an inset gateway that offered a set-back space for ne'er do wells that might choose to lie in wait.

Gabe let his jacket hang open, lifted the tail over the head of his tomahawk, put his hand on the grip of the pistol, bringing it to full cock as he held it under the flap of the jacket. He had a firm grip on the saddlebags on his shoulder and he kept his pace, yet watchful and anticipating anything. He caught the corner of a face peeking around the edge of the gateway setback, grinned at the brashness of the man and continued his pace, signaling Wolf to stay behind and to the side as they came close. When he drew near, three men stepped out to block his way. One held a belaying pin, slapping it in the palm of his left hand as he grinned at Gabe. The second held a long double-edged knife and the third, who stood in the middle and slightly ahead of the others, held a cocked pistol pointed casually at Gabe. The three had the look of sea-faring men, probably part of a mutinous crew of a river-running keel boat.

All were grinning at Gabe as the leader said, "We'll take that," nodding toward the saddlebags.

Gabe feigned surprise, "This," nodding toward the leather pouch, "what do you want with my dirty clothes?" He heard the low growl from Wolf and gave a flat palm sign at his side for the beast to stay. "I've heard of men gettin' desperate, but if you do my laundry, I'd be happy to pay you for your time," he offered, feigning sincerity and he put a hand to the bags.

"Don't try to be funny. We know what you've got in there, now hand it over or we'll take it off your dead body!" growled the leader, waving the barrel of the pistol side to side.

Gabe frowned, "Now fellas," he looked from one to the other, judging which appeared to be the greatest threat, "The last time I had a washer woman do my laundry, she charged extra cuz they stunk to high heaven. Are you sure you want to do this?"

"Shut up 'bout that! We know you got a thousand dollars in gold coin, and if you don't wanna die for that, hand it over!" demanded the leader, taking a slight step forward.

Gabe grinned, ducked his head slightly and reached for the bags, using the motion to hide his pulling of the pistol from his belt, and in one swift move, dropped the bags to the ground, pulled the weapon and fired the over/under pistol, the blast sending the big ball to shatter the sternum of the leader and smash through his backbone, instantly dropping the big man in a cloud of white smoke and splattering blood. The man with the belaying pin lunged forward but was met by the leaping black wolf, mouth open fangs showing, eyes flaring as he bit at the man's lower jaw and neck, locking his teeth into the flesh, knocking the attacker into the third man with the big knife and bearing them to the ground. As the knife wielder fought to gain his balance, Gabe quickly spun the second barrel of the pistol into place, brought the second hammer to full cock and brought the weapon to bear on the staggering rogue.

The man's eyes flared hatred, his left hand reaching for the fence to keep from falling, the muzzle of the pistol following his move, and as he caught himself, he stretched out his knife wielding hand, reaching for Gabe, but a simple side-step caused the man to fall forward, and Gabe brought the pistol down like a club to smash the man's skull, knocking him unconscious. The growls and snarls of Wolf brought Gabe's attention to his fellow defender, saw sightless eyes staring from the still body, and called to Wolf, "Enough boy, no!"

Wolf released his biting hold, stepped back as he glared at his prey, and turned to look at his friend, blood dripping from his jowls. Gabe spoke again, "Good boy, good boy, heel," and watched as the wolf came alongside and sat down on his haunches. Gabe looked at the two carcasses, the one unconscious man, shook his head and walked away. He thought on what happened, remembering the man had known and spoke about the thousand dollars in gold coin. There was only one way he would have known, and that was for the missing teller to have told them and either pointed him out or described him. Either way, the banker had been a part of the attack.

When he rounded the corner, he was surprised to see the large stone building with the sign across the top, "Choteau Trading Company," and Gabe was thoroughly impressed. This was the biggest and most impressive building in the town. The size alone told of the prosperity of the company and man, and the profitability of the fur trading business. He walked to the main door, stepped inside and went to the counter. A clerk with a slightly dingy linen shirt with gartered sleeves, looked up, "What can we do for you?" he asked, nothing friendly about his tone. His expression showing more aggravation than interest.

"I'd like to see Mr. Choteau, please," said Gabe, stepping to the counter and resting his elbow on the edge.

The clerk looked at Gabe, then down to Wolf, "Don't need that in here! What'chu need with Mr. Choteau?"

"He asked me to stop in when I came to town, so, I'm in town," explained Gabe.

The man looked him over with a critical eye, "Got'ny pelts?"

"No."

"Then you don't need to see him."

Gabe stepped closer, put both forearms on the counter and leaned toward the man. "Unless you want to mix it up a mite, I suggest you do as you're told. Now, tell him I'm here!" growled Gabe, already on his last bit of his patience. He had grown tired of the attitude of the city dwellers. "Look, friend, I've had my fill of you impudent and ill-mannered high and mighty nit wits. I've already left two dead bodies and one unconscious rogue in the street, and one more won't bother my conscience at all. You wanna be the one?"

The man backed up a step, eyes wide, and hands beginning to tremble, as he stuttered, "Uh, no, no-sir, not at all sir. But Mr. Choteau is not in, won't be in for a couple more days or so. He's coming in from one of our out-lying posts. Uh, you'll have to come back, sir."

Gabe nodded, "Now, wouldn't it have been easier to say that in the first place?"

"Uh, yes, yes-sir."

"Now, you got a sheriff, constable, or something in this town?" asked Gabe, anxious to account for the dead bodies.

"Uh, no sir. We had a town Marshall, but he up and left."

"Hmmm, all right. I'll be back." He spun on his heel and with a wave to Wolf, walked out the door and started to the livery.

***

Dusk was starting its retreat, yielding the vastness of the night to the lighting of the myriad of lanterns to decorate the night sky. The shadowy horseback figure walked up the long driveway, hunched slightly over the pommel of his saddle. The big shadow walked beside the buckskin as if the two had been life-long friends. As he neared the house, a graceful figure rose from the dark veranda, stepped to the edge and stood in the moonlight to wave Gabe close. As he neared, the fading dusk and the glow of the rising moon showed a different image than Elizabeth expected. She frowned, cocked her head to the side, "The horse looks familiar, but who's that in the saddle?"

Gabe chuckled, "One weary rider, searching for a place to lay his tired head."

"Well, I was about to offer you some left overs and some fresh coffee, but if you're that tired . . ."

"I'm never too tired for a good meal and hot coffee," he answered. He moved the horse to the hitch-rail, stepped down and walked up the steps to the veranda and dropped into a chair at the table. It was a cool but comfortable evening, and it was good to be home, he thought, then realized he already thought of this as home, and grinned.

Elizabeth sat beside him, looking at him and taking in the new image. The clean-shaven face, the haircut and the different clothes, gave the man an entirely new look. She slowly smiled and said, "I never would have recognized you. I like it!"

Gabe grinned, leaned back to allow Sophie to set the plate of food before him and watched as she poured the steaming coffee. He looked to Elizabeth, "It's nice to have a hot meal waiting. Haven't had that in a long time."

"Yes. You said you and Ezra had married sisters.

So, you married?"

"No. She was killed a while back. Earlier in the summer. That was part of what prompted this trip."

"I'm sorry. That must be hard to lose someone like that. What was her name?"

Gabe dropped his eyes, and began to explain, "The custom of her people, the Shoshone, and other native peoples, is to never mention the dead by name. They believe that will call up their spirit and not allow them to rest in peace. But, her name was Pale Otter. Her sister, Ezra's wife, is Grey Dove."

"You said you were married. How could you be married if you were out in the wilderness. Surely there aren't any ministers in the wild, are there?"

"There have been missionaries, priests and others that have gone into the wilderness long before this. Some as long as over a hundred years ago. The Spanish conquistadors often had a priest accompany them, and the catholic, both Spanish and French, had priests and friars that went among the natives long before English speaking trappers and explorers."

"And did one of those perform the wedding?" she asked, curious but not judgmental.

"No. We had a complete and formal native ceremony that involved the entire village. A very elaborate ceremony that started with cleansing sweat lodges and more. It's really quite an occasion, and to have a double ceremony with sisters, is even more so."

"Interesting. I would like to learn more about the ways of the natives, but some other time when we have more time." She leaned forward as he finished his meal and reached for the coffee cup, sat back and looked at her. "Did you get your business finished as you hoped?"

"Most of it. But Auguste wasn't back yet, so I'll need to make the trip again in a few days."

"Auguste?"

"Choteau, the man with the trading company."

"You know Auguste Choteau?"

"Of course, don't you?"

"Well, strictly on a social level. If you don't mind my asking, how does a man that spent the last five years in the wilderness know the most influential and prominent man in St. Louis?"

Gabe chuckled, "Oh, we met him when we were with the Osage Indians and I visited with him again just a few days back when I was on my way here. He's a good man, said he wanted to talk business with me at my convenience. So, I figured I'd hear what he had to say."

Elizabeth frowned slightly, looked at this man across the table from her, and said, "You are a very interesting man, Mr. Stone, yes you are."

"*Mr.* Stone? I thought we were on a first name basis, Elizabeth."

She smiled, "Yes we are, Gabe. Yes we are. But I believe there's a lot more to learn about you, am I right?"

He chuckled, "Isn't that true with most everyone?"

15 / Changes

Gabe had never worked on a farm, his home land in Philadelphia was pasture land for horses and little else. His youth had been spent roaming the woods with Ezra and tending to matters at school. Even the time at university had been devoted to studies and the summers were usually spent traveling abroad where he gained skill at boxing, fencing and in Japanese JuJutsu. But he was anxious to learn and be of help to this family that had welcomed him so readily. When he went to the main house for breakfast, he was herded into the dining room by a tousle headed Rupert as he stuffed his shirt in his trousers. "Take a seat!" he declared, nodding to the table. Sophie had already set the table with platters of steaming biscuits, pork belly, fried potatoes, a big bowl of milk gravy, and as he seated himself, she placed a platter of fried eggs in the middle of the table.

Gabe looked about, savoring the delightful aromas, and reached for a linen napkin just as the ladies swept into the room. Gabe scooted back the chair to stand and held the chair for Elizabeth as Rupert did for Eloise. "Good morning, ladies," Gabe greeted as he slid the chair forward for Elizabeth. The two couples set across from one another, no one seated at the ends of the long dining table, and Eloise smiled a somewhat mischievous smile as she nodded to Gabe's greeting.

As the men were seated, Rupert took Eloise's hand, nodded to Gabe and Elizabeth, "Let's ask the Lord's blessing, shall we?"

Gabe lowered his head and listened as Rupert asked a simple blessing of thanks for the bounty and the strength for the day. At his "Amen", Gabe echoed it and lifted his head to look upon the feast before him, "I certainly hope you don't set a table like this at every meal, if you do, I probably won't fit through the door before long!"

The others laughed, and Rupert said, "I think Sophie is expecting you to have a big appetite, what with being a genuine mountain man and all."

Gabe chuckled, "What she doesn't know is in the mountains, we don't have regular meal times and all too often we skip a meal or more, dependin'. . ."

Elizabeth looked at him and asked, "Depending?"

"Well, if you're getting chased by a war party of Indians bent on taking your hair, or if you're chasing slavers that have taken captives, or if you're tryin' to outrun a grizzly bear, you know, dependin' on circumstances." He grinned as he passed the platter of eggs.

Elizabeth paused, turned to look at him, and said, "Surely, you're joshing!"

Gabe grinned, "Well, we don't do that every day..." and chuckled.

"Have you run into a grizzly bear? And are they as big as they say?"

Gabe grinned, "A time or two, and let's see," he looked around, saw the ceiling beam that separated the dining room from the kitchen area, "that beam up there," pointing to the beam, "That's about six feet, maybe more. If a big grizz was standing on his hind feet, that beam would be about here," putting his arm across his chest at the point of the sternum, "on him. And if he was of a mind, he could break that beam with one swipe of his paw!"

Elizabeth's eyes squinted as she looked at Gabe, "I don't believe that! And what would they be doing on their hind feet? Don't they go around like other bears on all fours?"

Gabe grinned, sipped at his coffee. "Yes, they do, but when they get mad, they're kinda like a mad woman, they rise up on their hind feet and start slappin'!" and he ducked as Elizabeth took a swipe at him. "See! Just like that!"

Everyone laughed, and Gabe added, "Don't let me

forget, and after we eat I'll show you a necklace Pale Otter made for me out of the claws of one of those itty-bitty grizzlies." He smiled and said, "Pass the biscuits, please."

Elizabeth looked across the table to her brother, "Didn't I hear you say one time that those mountain men are all big liars!" and glanced to Gabe.

Gabe spoke up before Rupert could answer, "We gotta be! If'n we told the truth you'd find that harder to believe than a little white lie!"

Elizabeth giggled into her napkin, smiled and said, "I don't know if I can ever believe you again. Here, have some potatoes," and handed Gabe the dish.

Gabe looked at Rupert, "I noticed in town there was a Catholic church, but I didn't see any other. Are there other church buildings around?" "No, not yet. We have had some itinerant preachers come through now and then and hold services wherever they could, but, I don't know, I guess most folks around here haven't been too concerned about spiritual matters. Even the Catholic priest has a hard time drawing a crowd, even though there are many Spaniards and Frenchmen that profess to be Catholic, and the Spanish had restrictions regarding Protestant gatherings, so. . ." mused Rupert, shrugging.

"And you folks? I appreciated the prayer, so I felt comfortable asking, but do you have anyone around that has a church service?"

"There was a group over in St. Charles for a while,

but I haven't heard anything lately. And there was a group south of town, the area they're calling Carondelet, but nothing nearer."

"What about you, Gabe, are you a Christian?" asked Eloise.

Gabe smiled, nodded, "Yes ma'am. When I was a youngster in short pants, my family attended Christ Church and my best friend's father was a pastor, so between the two, I learned about the need to receive Christ as my Savior, but never took that step until my friend Ezra encouraged me and showed me what was necessary. Since that time, the Lord has always been by my side."

Elizabeth grew a little contemplative, lifted her eyes to Eloise, and glanced to Gabe. "What Eloise is concerned about is the welfare of my soul. I have not come to that place or time when I find it necessary to depend on anyone or anything but myself. I have sometimes thought that those who turn to God are usually weak or on the superstitious side of things."

Everyone sat silent for a moment until Gabe turned to look at Elizabeth, "What was it in your life that caused you to become so cynical?" he asked, softly.

Elizabeth dropped her eyes to her hands that twisted the napkin in her lap, and Gabe added, "I'm sorry, it's not my place to be so intrusive. Perhaps some other time we can have a discussion, as you wish or not. But," he paused, pushed his coffee cup and plate back, stood, and said, "I promised to show you something." He smiled, nodded, and walked out.

When he returned, the table had been cleared and the three were silent, but it was evident they had been talking. They looked up as Gabe walked to the table and lay before them the necklace given him by the Arapaho chief, Sitting Elk. Gabe unfolded the piece of buckskin to reveal a necklace that held two bear claws with tufts of white hair at their base. The claws were over four inches long and at the base were a creamy white but melded to a glossy black at the tip. The claws rested on a red felt pad, surrounded by colored quills, and hung from a multi-colored coral necklace. He lay it on the table before them and each one leaned forward to look more closely. Elizabeth reached out and gently touched the claws, looked up at Gabe, "Are these from a grizzly?"

Gabe grinned, "No, those are from what they call a Spirit Bear. It's a bear that is rarely seen in the northern Rockies, a creamy white in color and a little smaller than a grizzly. That was given to me by the chief of the Arapaho nation, Chief Sitting Elk, when he gave me my name. Spirit Bear."

"You have an Indian name? Spirit Bear?" enthusiastically asked Elizabeth, smiling broadly.

"Ummhmmm. He gave both Ezra and me our names, Ezra is called Black Buffalo. It's an honor to be given a name by the native peoples and is usually done after some special happening or other."

"Oh? And what did you do?" asked Elizabeth.

"That's not important," he said as he lay another piece of folded buckskin down and unfolded it to reveal the grizzly claw necklace.

"Ohhh, my," began Elizabeth as she looked and touched the long claws. "These are grizzly?" Gabe nodded. "Otter made that for me from the paws of a big ol' silvertip."

Elizabeth frowned, not understanding.

"A silvertip is an older grizzly, their long fur is kinda like an old man with grey hair, only just the tips." He looked at the one remaining platter that still held some biscuits, "If he was to put his paw on that platter, it would be totally covered."

The three looked at the platter, back to a sober faced Gabe, and each one frowned slightly as they tried to determine if he was being truthful. He reached down and lay the necklace under the platter to show the length of the claws protruding from under, and they lifted their eyebrows in surprise. Rupert asked, "And, did the bear die? Because he was old, I mean?"

Gabe grinned, "No, he died of lead poisoning."

Rupert quickly understood, chuckled, and when Eloise and Elizabeth looked at him, he explained, "Lead poisoning, too many bullets!"

The women smiled, shaking their heads and Eloise muttered, "Men!"

***

For three days the men worked the farm. The crops needed thinning and weeding, horses needed work as several were two-year olds that had not been broken to ride but Rupert had his way of gentling the animals and preferred to do that himself. They were long but rewarding days and at supper of the third day Gabe said, "I need to go into town tomorrow. Think you can do without my help for a day?"

"Oh, I'm reasonably certain I can manage," answered Rupert with a jovial grin as he forked another bite of mulligan stew into his mouth.

Gabe grinned, did the same, and after a sip of coffee, added, "Choteau asked me to stop by and he wasn't back the other day, so, thought I'd go see what he had on his mind."

Rupert looked up at him as he lifted another forkful, pausing and asked, "Choteau? Are you talking about Jean Pierre or Auguste?"

"Auguste. I've not met Jean Pierre. I assume they're brothers?"

"Half-brother, I believe." chuckled Rupert as he thought about them, "They are sometimes called the 'River Barons', because of their many business interests and dealings."

"Well, I only thought it to be the courteous thing to do, since he asked. But, I'm not into becoming a

'River Baron' or anything like it! I've little left to do, check with the postman to see if there might be correspondence for me, perhaps from my sister, and see if she needs anything. Then, it's just wait for spring and head back to the mountains."

"Oh? You're determined to return to the mountains?" asked Elizabeth, trying to appear nonchalant, but failing, as she fidgeted with her napkin, what appeared to be a habit with her.

"Yes'm. My heart is in the wilderness, the mountains that stretch to the blue of the sky, the clear blue canopy that seldom holds clouds, the vast distances, and to walk where white men have never been before, just does somethin' to me. It's hard to explain to someone that has never seen it."

Elizabeth had watched his eyes glaze over as he pictured the wild western lands, cocked her head to the side to try to see within and maybe understand the wanderlust of the man, but she had no common point of reference from which to imagine his wild adventures and journeys. She sighed heavily, asked, "Excuse me please. I think I'll go to the veranda for some evening air."

The others watched her go, then Gabe got up to follow.

16 / Proposition

It was a frosty morning that greeted Gabe as he rolled from his blankets. He grabbed his jacket as he went from the cabin to his chosen place for his morning time with the Lord, the small clearing on the knob of a hill that overlooked the pasture. The gossamer clouds lay low on the meadow, the dim light of early morning giving an ethereal look to the land. And the hush that accompanied the mist gave a strange comfort as he seated himself on the log and bowed his head.

***

The leaves hung with the dampness dripping from their leaves as he made his way to the house, his boots wet from the dew in the grass. He stomped his feet on the stone steps, went to the door and before he could knock, it was opened to reveal a smiling Elizabeth.

"Come in, come in! This is such a dreary day; you need some hot coffee!" and led the way to the dining room, where a bountiful breakfast was already laid out.

Gabe grinned at the jovial mood of the woman, "You're certainly in a fine mood today!"

She smiled as she was seated, looked at Gabe as he seated himself, "So, you're going into town today?" she asked.

Gabe frowned slightly, suspecting something, but answered, "That's the plan."

"Would you like some company? I have some shopping I could do, and we could take the buggy. That way, while you conduct your business, I can get around town and do mine!" She smiled prettily as if the subject was closed and she would broker no argument.

Gabe slowly lifted his head, and looked across the table to Rupert and Eloise, who was trying her best to keep from laughing, then looked back to Elizabeth, "And just when do *we* depart on this little shopping trip?"

"Well, right after breakfast, of course. Don't you have much to do?"

Gabe nodded as he accepted the proffered biscuits from a somber faced Rupert. Both men slightly shook their heads, knowing they were outnumbered, and nothing could be done. It would be best just to accept the situation and try to make the best of it.

***

Their first stop was at the mercantile which also doubled as the postman and Gabe was pleased to have a letter from his sister and another from the Attorney Sutterfield. While Elizabeth moseyed around the store, looking and examining the goods, Gabe stepped outside to take a seat on a bench by the window and read his missives.

After the initial greetings, Gwyneth continued, *Now, my dear brother, it was very kind of you to offer additional finances, but father and I had this discussion before you ever left. My husband has a very lucrative position and we want for nothing. Father knew you would be best at handling the finances from his estate and he put his trust in you, therefore I am in total agreement with his directives and know you will tend to any situation that may arise and if I should ever be in need, well, you are just a letter away. However, I have the utmost confidence in my beloved husband and am very happy in our lovely home in Washington. I am certain the future is bright for us and you will hear about his success.* She continued with remarks about mutual acquaintances and other trivia that was of little interest. He folded the letter, slipped it into his jacket and opened the correspondence from the lawyer.

As we agreed, I have settled your father's estate, the last detail being the disposition of the property. I was pleased to purchase the property and the agreed upon annual sum will be deposited in your account here in Philadelphia. At your request, I transferred the stipulated sum to the new branch of the Bank of North America in St. Louis. And of course, that leaves a considerable account that you may draw upon at any time, here in the main bank in Philadelphia.

I must also caution you. Mr. Jedediah Wilson has not given up on his vengeful ways and has increased the bounty on your head to $5,000.00. Although his health is failing, his anger has only increased. He is said to be quite disagreeable with anyone in his employ and family. His vengeance is like a canker that eats away at him, and although his wife's brother, the honorable Mr. Rutledge of the Supreme Court has warned him of his unlawful posting, he continues. My concern is Mr. Wilson has many contacts, even among those at the bank, and might become aware of your whereabouts through those acquaintances.

Gabe skimmed the remainder of the letter, shook his head and stuffed it into his pocket with the other, remembering the attempt by the teller and his friends when he was set upon by the rogues that knew of his withdrawal from the bank. But the one question about the Wilson's that was given by the bank manager, was the one that bothered him the most.

***

"So, you see, young Mr. Stone, you would be doing me

a great service to serve as guide and hunter to the expedition," declared Auguste Choteau as he sipped his ale in the Inn at the corner of Second and Spruce. They sat at the corner table beside the lone window which offered a fly-specked and distorted view of the riverfront.

"I understand your wish to have a trading post as far north on the Missouri as possible, but that would be a long way to pole a keel boat. And there's a definite point the boats could not pass, there's several falls that would prevent passage," answered Gabe, looking at the man known as one of the 'River Barons' for his daring in business.

"You said the furthest post you saw was among the Mandans, is that right?"

"Yes, but there was also the Northwest post, Fort Mackay at the confluence with the Knife River," reiterated Gabe, leaning back in his chair, considering the proposal of the Choteau traders.

"And no others?" queried Choteau.

"No, not established posts, anyway. Although there were a couple men that spent a winter with the Kootenai. I believe they said they had been with Clamorgan's company of Discoverers. And of course I told you about Alexander Henry and Thompson at the headwaters of the Missouri."

"But they didn't establish a post and you said they were leaving, right?"

"Yes."

"And they came by land from the Saskatchewan river country and the Northwest company." He spoke as if he was calculating and scheming. Then lifted his eyes to Gabe again, "Marvelous! Then it's wide open for us. If we can get our boats past the Mandans, into the land of the Hidatsa and the Assiniboine, maybe the Crow, it would be rich trading country. People that would welcome traders and their goods." He smiled as he thought of the possibilities, sobered his expression and sipped at his ale as he thought.

He leaned forward to place his elbows on the table, lowered his voice and started, "Now, if you're willing, here's what I want to do . . ." He carefully laid out his plans for the outfitting of at least one keelboat and crew, perhaps two. He had ordered the craft from a boat maker in Pittsburgh known for his excellent craftsmanship in the making of the river boats. Harald Brackenridge, whose brother was a state legislator, had established himself as a skilled boat maker, and when the whiskey rebellion gave rise to bootleggers and river pirates, his business of making keelboats prospered.

The boats were due to arrive any day, loaded with iron goods, whiskey, and more, from the Pittsburgh stove works and the many distillers. The goods would be welcomed by the many settlers in the area, and the profit would outfit the expedition to the territories.

"What about crew and traders?" asked Gabe.

"I believe most would stay on, although some would

need to be replaced. And I have some experienced traders that worked in my other posts, like the one you last visited that the Spanish Governor wanted closed."

"Won't the Spanish be just as difficult to deal with regarding any other posts, especially any that are further into the territory?" asked Gabe, unfamiliar with the governmental dealings.

Choteau grinned, "I don't believe so. I have recently been informed that it might soon come to pass that the Spaniards will surrender their control, but that's on the hush hush, you understand."

Gabe nodded, frowned, "If I were to agree, will there be room on board for two horses and my gear? Or do you expect me to be afoot?"

"No, no. Of course not. As per my design, there will be space aboard for at least four horses, if needed. And you will probably spend most of your time ashore, hunting meat for the crew and scouting the natives."

"And you expect to depart early spring?"

"That's right. The earliest possible. The river between here and the confluence with the Kaw, or the Kansas, will be easiest, although the fullest in spring. After that, when the river turns north, there will be few riverside paths for the cordelle crew and the going will be more of a challenge."

They spent another hour discussing the details of the crew and other needed personnel as well as supplies and trade goods. Gabe's insight with the northern plains people was valuable to Choteau, realizing the needs or wants of those people varied somewhat from the tribes in the territory nearer the Mississippi. As they rose to leave, Choteau said, "My brother and I are giving a soiree at our home, Friday next. Won't you and your lady companion join us? Her brother and his wife would also be welcome."

Gabe raised one eyebrow, "It's been sometime since I've been to such a gathering." He looked down at his duds and up to Choteau, "And I'm afraid I have yet to procure the appropriate attire."

Choteau grinned, reached into his pocket for a card, handed it to Gabe, "Here is the name of my tailor. If you stop by today, tell him I sent you, he should have a suitable outfit for you by, oh, mid-week I'd imagine."

Gabe grinned, "Then we'll be happy to join you."

The men parted, Gabe turning towards the central business section of town, having agreed to meet Elizabeth at her millinery shop on Third. It was a short walk and he was in a contemplative mood as he strolled and was almost taken by surprise when two men stepped from between two stone buildings directly behind him. But he heard the brush of leather against stone and the thud of boots on the boardwalk and ducked and spun around. The belaying pin, a favorite with shoulder strikers from the east and men that had spent time aboard ship, swished through the air, connecting with nothing and causing the striker to stumble forward into the fist of Gabe that he brought up from the ground and buried in the man's midriff. The second man was startled and stepped back bringing up a pistol. Gabe heard the hammer cock as it was lifted, but he pushed the bent over striker into the second man, forcing them both against the stone wall.

Gabe brought up his knee into the groin of the first man, grabbed the hand of the second, twisting the pistol from his grip as he pulled him over the back of his friend. As his weight bore down on the moaning man that clutched his crotch, Gabe twisted his arm behind him, showing no mercy as he wrenched it from his shoulder socket. Both men fell face forward onto the boardwalk, groaning and whining. Gabe spoke softly, "Thank you gentlemen. I needed a bit of a work out. Perhaps next time, you'll be a bit more careful as to who you try."

He stepped away from them with a quick glance over his shoulder at the two as they writhed on the walkway. Both men glared at the back of Gabe as he departed, walking briskly and beginning to whistle a joyous tune.

It was at Millicent's Millinery Shop that Gabe found Elizabeth, settling her account at the counter with a large parcel beside her. She looked up at him, saw his broad smile, and asked, "I take it everything went according to your wishes?"

"Oh, you mean my whistling? Oh no, it's because *you* have not finished *your* shopping!" he declared as

142   B.N. RUNDELL

he stepped to her side.

She frowned, "But I have."

"And do you have an outfit for the soiree at the Choteau's Friday next?" he asked, smiling broadly and leaning on the counter.

Her eyes flared, then squinted, "Mr. Stone, would you be joshing me again?"

"Absolutely not! We have been invited, as has your brother and his bride, to a special event at the home of Auguste and Jean Pierre Choteau, Friday next."

She looked at him, cocked her head to the side as if to examine his motives more clearly, and then said, "Alright. But if I find you are joshing me, *you* will pay for this dress!"

"Happy to m'lady, happy to. Now, if you'll excuse me, I have to go to the haberdashery and order my suit. I will call for you shortly." He turned, gave a slight bow, and left the shop. Elizabeth turned to Millicent, "Well, I guess I need a new gown!" smiling broadly.

17 / Soiree

Rupert stood as Gabe came from his cabin, the men looking at one another with surprise. Neither appeared as they had in the previous days, always attired in linen trousers, boots, drop shoulder shirts and work jackets. Now they were outfitted for the coming event in town. Gabe wore brown breeches, long socks, spatterdashes and buckle shoes, topped by a tan waistcoat over the loose-fitting linen shirt. A cravat at his throat had a loose bow that hung to his chest, and the only familiar garment was his beaded and fringed buckskin jacket. He looked up at Rupert, standing with one hand on a porch post. He also had breeches but his were black and contrasted with the grey waistcoat. His buckle shoes and spatterdashes were black, socks crème colored, and his shirt and cravat were also white. His grey greatcoat lay over the porch rail, and he watched Gabe mount the steps to the veranda.

Rupert grinned, "So, you ready for this big event?" as he turned to the door.

Gabe chuckled, "Is a man ever really ready to take a lady dancing?"

As soon as they stepped into the room, they were brought to a halt by the ladies that stood side by side, smiling and waiting for the men's approval. Gabe looked to Elizabeth who wore a stunning high waisted pale cream-colored floor-length dress. A pattern of tiny flowers had been hand stitched in a gold thread and was accented by a thin gold band that circled her form just below her breasts. The scoop neck showed a puffed handkerchief at the bust line, and the long sleeves tapered to a tight cuff at the wrist. The toes of tan leather slippers showed beneath the hem. Gabe smiled as he nodded, bowed slightly, and looked directly at Elizabeth, "You are absolutely radiant!" She curtsied, smiled and extended her hand for him to take.

Eloise had a simple yet elegant cotton muslin dress with a woven pattern of varying widths of stripes over the short sleeve and at the bustline and hem. A wide belt of white satin rested just below her breasts, accenting the simplicity and elegance of the gown. She smiled coyly at Rupert, who immediately stepped forward to take her hand, "Madam, may I escort you to the affair this evening?" She smiled, and stepped closer, whispered something in his ear that brought a blush to his neck, and they stepped to the door.

***

The ladies were quite excited about the event, and Elizabeth shared that it had been well over a year since they had any occasion to dress up and go to town, and this was the first time they had been invited into the Choteau home. They were considered the elite of the community since it was Auguste Choteau and his stepfather, Pierre Laclède, that were the founders of St. Louis, while Auguste and his half- brother Jean-Pierre had built their very successful trading business. The Choteau home was the most impressive mansion in St. Louis, situated on the Southwest corner of Main and Washington streets and surrounded by shoulder high stone wall. Standing a full two stories high with a third floor shown by two large dormers, both floors were surrounded by covered verandas with white railings. Two massive chimneys, one mid-way and one at the north end, stood tall above the peaked and painted red shingled roof.

As the buggy pulled into the roadway and to the foot of the wide stairs, a colored man outfitted in black and white with white gloves, took the reins of the horses and held them while the men stepped down, then helped the ladies to step down. As they mounted the stairs, the groom took the buggy to the barn, watched by Gabe as he looked over the property. Although the structure was near the corner of the property, this was not the typical city block. The property stretched further north into a wooded area that also bent back to the west. The land was slightly elevated and offered a broad view of the city below.

As they neared the door, it swung wide and Auguste was waiting, smiling, and extended his hand, "Welcome, welcome! Come right in. Here, let Jefferson take your wraps." He paused, looked at the ladies, made a slight bow, "Ladies, may I welcome you to my home. I am René Auguste Choteau."

Gabe stepped forward, "Auguste, this is Elizabeth Haines, and this is Rupert Haines and his wife, Eloise."

Each of the ladies offered their hand and he took it with a slight bow, "Very pleased to meet you ladies," then turned to Rupert and extended his hand, "I believe I've met you before, haven't I?" he asked as they shook hands.

"Yes, we've met at your trading house," answered Rupert.

"Good, good. Now, if you will follow me. We'll go right into the ball room, there's a roaring fire where you can warm up."

As they stepped into the larger room, they were greeted by Choteau's wife and he introduced her, "Ladies and gentlemen, this is my lovely wife, Marie Therese." He turned to his wife, "Marie, this is Gabe Stone, and Rupert Haines, his wife Eloise and his sister, Elizabeth."

The ladies curtsied to one another, and Marie nodded to both men, but did not extend her hand. With a broad smile, she spoke to the ladies, "Let's us go to the fire, it's much nicer there," and led the women away. The room was about twenty by forty feet, with the fireplace at one end and windows along the long side at the back of the house. The opposite end from the fireplace four young men were readying their musical instruments for the evening, two violinists, a flutist, and one seated at the bench before a harpsicord.

As the ladies distanced themselves from the men, Auguste explained, "My brother, Jean-Pierre, and his wife will join us shortly. We'll dine and if everyone is of a mind, we'll dance a bit. My wife has been wanting to have a soiree for some time, says she doesn't want to get shut in come winter time." The men chuckled at the thought but before anything else could be said, Jean-Pierre and his wife, Constance, joined them, just before the servants called, "Dinner is served."

***

Dinner was a sumptuous affair with copious amounts and varieties of food, a much more extravagant layout than Gabe had seen since the days in Philadelphia, and more than Rupert and the ladies had ever seen. Most of the conversation was carried on by the women, but once the meal was completed, the men excused themselves to the veranda when both brandy and cigars were offered. But Gabe chose not to partake, preferring the clear air to the cigars, and having never developed a taste for spirits, he politely declined and accepted a cup of steaming black coffee.

"So, my brother tells me you have been to the headwaters of the Missouri and beyond, is that right?" began Jean-Pierre, stepping to the side of Gabe as both men leaned against the pillared railing.

"That's correct," answered Gabe, expecting some kind of inquiry regarding his time in the territory. After Auguste's proposal, he knew there would be questions and he willingly listened.

"And what tribes have you been among?" inquired the younger Choteau.

"All of 'em. Except for those in the far northwest, but I will."

Jean-Pierre was somewhat taken aback at the man's simple answers yet surprised to learn where he had been.

For a while, the men talked of the different natives, their lands and their ways, but Rupert could only listen and learn. When Jean-Pierre was satisfied as to Gabe's knowledge and experience, he asked, "Do you think we can establish a post among the tribes at the headwaters?"

Gabe grinned, "It's not so much the tribes, as how to get there. There are several insurmountable falls in the north bend of the Missouri that drop forty to eighty feet and the canyon walls beside them are solid rock and over a hundred feet high. I told your brother that there have been traders from the Northwest company and Hudson's Bay company that have traded with the Kootenai, Salish, Blackfoot, Gros Ventre, but none established a post."

"I see. But do you think we can build a fort further north than any exist today?"

"Probably. Depending on the mood of the people at the time. I have found the northern plains Indians to be a little less trusting than others, like the Osage, Otoe, Kansa, and even the Ponca. Although most have traded with the French or Spanish at some time in the past."

The men were interrupted when Jean-Pierre's wife, Constance, summoned them to the dance floor. The musicians had been warming up and the ladies were anxious to get on the floor. Marie-Therese took charge and positioned the four couples in a square, facing one another, and gave the first instructions. "Now, for the *contredanse allemande* there will be several changes, each one being to the count of four. The first will be a simple circle, followed by a figure eight for each couple, and the next ..." and she continued through the instructions for the first four changes, then asked the musicians to begin. They started with a number by J.S. Bach from his *English Suites*.

Although the dance style was supposed to be sophisticated and formal, the lack of experience and skill, especially on the part of the men, lent a certain hilarity to the evening and before long, everyone was laughing and having a good time. After they somewhat mastered the first four changes, Marie-Therese introduced four more, and the stumbling and laughing began again. However, before the evening was over, the four couples had gained a certain adroitness with the moves and changes and seemed to make it through an entire number without too many mistakes.

After just over an hour of dancing, everyone was tired and ready to call it quits. Gabe and company expressed their thankfulness and appreciation for an exceptional evening and the Choteau's all said they must do it again and soon. As they mounted the buggy, they brought out the blankets and Gabe picked the grizzly pelt from the back and the two couples bundled up for the ride home by the light of the full moon. It had been a pleasant evening and everyone had thoroughly enjoyed themselves, but Gabe was a little concerned at the way Elizabeth seemed to be drawing closer to him and showing a special fondness that he wasn't quite ready for, but it was pleasant, nevertheless.

18 / Preparations

"There she is!" declared Choteau. They were standing on the stone wall that separated the wharf from the town and overlooking the waterfront. Lying alongside the only stone pier was a keelboat, rocking in the water as it tugged at its lines. "She's forty-six feet, bow to stern, has a twelve-foot beam, four-foot depth and draws about twenty-four inches," he stood with arms crossed and grinning like a proud papa. "Designed her myself!" He turned to look at Gabe, "Let's go down and have a closer look."

Gabe nodded, motioned for Choteau to lead the way, and they went to the steps, and walked across the rocky shore toward the wharf. The craft was a well-made boat with space in the bow holding benches for rowers and in the stern that held a small corral for horses. Atop the long cabin sat a cook stove in a square of sand before the mast. Behind the mast was a cleated area for the helmsman, or *Patron*, to maneuver the long rudder. Along the side were cleated walkways for the crewmen when it was necessary to utilize poling. The cabin was to house the cargo, a maximum of thirty tons. Two men came from the cabin at the hail of Choteau and stepped to the wharf, hands outstretched to greet the two visitors.

Choteau turned to Gabe, "This is Phillipe Galvez, a family friend from New Orleans. He'll be the *Patron*, or master, and will be the man in charge. Once they reach the location for a post, he'll also be the trader." He turned toward the second man, "This is Etienne Duplessis. He will be the *bosseman,* or bowsman." He motioned to Gabe as he spoke to the men, "This is Gabe Stone. He'll be the guide and hunter, most of his time will be spent on shore, but he's the one that knows the Indians and can speak their language. He's the man that will keep you out of trouble, if possible."

"Then I definitely want to be friends with you," declared Phillipe, extending his hand to shake. Gabe shook his hand, looking the man over as he did. Although unimpressive at first, for he was quite average in appearance, dark hair, black eyes, sallow complexion, and of average size, the man's handshake was firm and he looked directly into Gabe's eyes, his gaze piercing and unyielding. Gabe slowly lifted his head as he looked at the man, pleased with the confidence that emanated from him. He was a man that would readily take control and although not very big, would probably be formidable in any conflict.

"Oui! Me too," declared Etienne, also leaning forward with his hand extended. Gabe readily took his hand, only to see his disappear in the massive mitt of the very large man. Standing at least four or five inches over six feet, appearing almost as broad, the deep chested man would easily weigh close to two hundred fifty pounds, and none of it fat. But his broad smile and soft eyes showed a kindness that belied his size, yet his firm handshake told of a man that was aware of his strength and size. Gabe grinned up at the man and said, "Your name was mountain?"

"No, no. Etienne!" he answered, then realizing what Gabe had implied, he laughed with a laugh that seemed to vibrate the wharf itself. His deep voice was as big as his stature but there was nothing intimidating about the man's personality.

The others chuckled at the 'mountain' reference, and the four men stepped back aboard the keelboat for Choteau to show Gabe around. Simple in design, it was an impressive craft for Gabe to examine. Although he had been acquainted with keelboats from his trip down the Ohio River, the only ones he had seen were in the hands of river pirates and he never had a close-up look, at least not when he wasn't shooting at those aboard.

When they stepped up atop the long cabin, Choteau showed him a feature he designed, "This is the mast, what I call a collapsible mast. See here," and he pointed to what appeared to be a long tongue and groove joint about two feet above the top of the cabin, "these pins are removeable and the mast can be lain down forward. Whenever the craft is being cordelled and the trees overhang the water, they often get entangled with the mast. This way, it can be lowered, and the towing is easier. And when the wind picks up and a sail can be used, then they can raise the mast and use it."

They walked to the forward edge of the cabin and Choteau motioned to the benches, "Those are for the rowers when they can be used. There are also oar locks at the fore and aft edges of the *passe avant,* or the running boards." He pointed to the narrow walkway on either side of the cabin. "Phillipe will be the helmsman," pointing to the long-handled rudder, "And Etienne will be in the bow. His job is to look out for anything in the water, make sure the rope that goes through that metal loop," pointing to the metal loop at the tip of tip of the prow, "doesn't get fouled."

Gabe looked around as they stepped down from the cabin, and asked Choteau, "How much cargo you gonna be takin'?"

"Well, most of it will be trade goods, some supplies, but we'll be counting on you to supply most of the meat. So, trade goods, twenty to thirty tons. I've got a list started I'd like you to look over."

"And how soon you plannin' on pullin' out?" asked Gabe, looking at the sky as if he could discern the weather.

"Well, this is March. I'm hopin' we can be on the

water, oh, mid-April, depending on the weather."

"Do you have all your crew?" asked Gabe as they stepped to the wharf.

"We do. They're housed at the St. Louis Exchange, but they'll be busy tending to the boat, fresh caulking, finishing, cleaning and such. Then we'll start loading. If the weather breaks sooner, we'll leave sooner."

"So, my horses will be on board?"

"As you need. I'm thinking you won't need to be hunting until after you pass the Kansas confluence, but that will be up to you. And whenever you want to rest up your horses, bring 'em back aboard and take a day or so."

"Sounds like you've got things well in control. I didn't think the time would pass so quickly, but I'm ready to get back to the mountains." He shook hands with Choteau, bid him good bye and went to the livery to fetch his horse and Wolf and return to the farm. He enjoyed the solitary time with Wolf and the Buckskin, it gave him time to think, remember, and consider. He *was* anxious to get back to the mountains, the city and all these people were part of his past, a past best left behind him. The five months with the Haines had been pleasant enough, but every day in the presence of Elizabeth was getting more and more uncomfortable. She had made it known that she didn't want him to leave and had done everything she could to convince him to stay, but it just wasn't in him to return to the lifestyle demanded of a married man in the city. But there was something he wanted to talk to her about, but for now, it would have to wait.

His arrangement with Choteau was for a percentage of the profits from the trading post. But he also wanted that percentage to be deposited to the account of the Haines, although they did not know of Gabe's arrangement. Gabe knew he had no need of the funds, being well provided for by his father's estate, and he knew the Haines had a few difficult years behind them and possibly more yet to come, farming is an uncertain concern. And with Elizabeth without a husband and an uncertain future, it would be good for her to have independent means. And, it might make Gabe's conscience a little less convicting.

Gabe looked every bit the country gentleman when he stepped through the door of the Bank of North America on the corner of Second Street and Chestnut. It had been a few months since his first visit and he wanted to ascertain the intentions the manager, Philip Dorman. When the teller looked up to see Gabe standing before him, he unconsciously took a step back, regained his composure, and tried to appear nonchalant as he asked, "May I help you, sir?" without looking directly at Gabe.

"Mr. Dorman, please," stated Gabe, stepping back from the counter to await the teller opening the gate to admit him.

The teller nodded, went to the door, rapped twice

and opened and stepped in, returning momentarily to say, "Mr. Dorman will see you now, sir."

Gabe stepped through the gate, looking at the teller who still refused to look at him. As Gabe stepped into the office, he was greeted by the manager, who motioned for him to take a seat as he said, "Mr. Stonecroft, so good to see you." Once he was seated, he shuffled a few papers to look important, then looked up at Gabe.

Gabe grinned, having waited for the man to look at him, and began, "Mr. Dorman, my attorney, Mr. Sutterfield, you recall?"

"Yes, yes, of course."

"He explained to me that the question you used that referenced the Wilson family, was not a part of his correspondence. He also said you came from the Philadelphia office and still have contacts in that city, is that correct?"

"Uh, well, yes, I suppose it is, but I don't understand . . ." he began but was stopped by the upheld hand of Gabe.

"Simply this, after my last visit, I was confronted by three men that already knew about the one thousand dollars in gold coin that I carried," Gabe paused to watch the reaction of the man, and continued as Dorman began to fidget and shuffle more papers. "The only way they could have known is if you or your teller," he nodded toward the outer room, "had told the brigands and suggested they take it from me. Now, as you have probably been made aware, they were unsuccessful."

Gabe scooted forward on the chair, leaned forward

to rest his forearms on the edge of Dorman's desk and continued, "Now, as you are also probably aware, there are certain individuals that, contrary to the law, wish me harm. I will be leaving St. Louis soon, and if anyone even thinks about coming after me, or doing harm to those that are near to me, I will take care of them first, then, Mr. Dorman, I will come after you and your little friend out there." He paused, sat back, and added, "Do we understand each other?"

Dorman tried to replace his expression of shock and fear with one of indignation by taking a deep breath and pursing his lips as he leaned forward, "Mr. Stonecroft, I am insulted that you would even think that I or anyone that works for me would be anything but honest and reputable. We would never . . ." but he was interrupted by Gabe as he stood, leaned on the edge of the desk and glared at the man, "You best remember what I said, and as you started to say, 'you would never', would be words for you to *live* by," and the emphasis put on the word 'live' conveyed a much stronger message. Gabe straightened up, smiled, turned and walked out of the bank, grinning all the while.

If there was to be a confrontation with any of Wilson's bounty hunters, he wanted it over and done with before he left on the keelboat. But he also wanted no harm to come to any of the Haines family, so he knew he was going to have to be doubly vigilant for the next few weeks before he took to the river.

19 / Conspirators

O'Reilly's Pub sat in a two-story red brick building on the corner of First and Pine. In the corner with a small window facing the river and another facing Pine street, it had become a favorite of dock workers and business men alike. On this day, seated by the window, were five men, four roughly attired, one in a business suit and looking very uncomfortable and out of place. One man, apparently the leader of the four, sat elbow to elbow with the nervous well-attired chap and between slugs from his beaker of rum, he jostled the business man with his elbow.

"Now, Dorman, old man Wilson sent us, and we've come a long ways and a mighty long time to get this far, so, give us the low down on where we can find this Stonecroft." He took another long draught from his mug, wiped his mouth with his tattered and dirty sleeve, and glared at the man beside him.

"What assurances do I have that I will get my share?" muttered Dorman, looking around somewhat furtively.

"Not my problem. You get yours from Wilson, just like we'uns."

"But if Stonecroft knows I've told you, and you don't take him, he said he would come after me. If it gets out about my telling, then I'll be ruined!"

The leader, who gave his name as Frank Foley, chuckled, looked at his friends as they joined in the laughter, and turned back to Dorman, "Ain't no way this one man is gonna get away from us! One city-bred mamma's boy that scored a lucky shot in a duel ain't nuthin' to be afraid of anyway!"

"You don't understand, there were three that tried to take him, and he killed two and seriously injured the other. They didn't lay a hand on him! Now, does that sound like a mamma's boy?" protested Dorman, fidgeting with the leather case on his lap.

"Oh he did, did he? Well, them was just no-account city lay-abouts, prob'ly never took anybody that wasn't drunk, so I still don't see a problem. Now, what can you tell us?"

He sighed heavily, leaned forward and pointed out the window, "See that keelboat yonder?" and looked at the men as they craned to see through the fly-specked and distorted glass. "That boat is going up the Missouri for the Choteau's, and your Mr. Stonecroft, will be going with them."

"So, when they goin'?" growled Foley, looking back at Dorman.

"As soon as the weather allows. From what I hear, sometime within the next few weeks," he proclaimed, leaning back in his seat as if that was sufficient information for the men.

"We ain't waitin' weeks!" growled the man across the table, the biggest and grimiest of the four.

Foley frowned at the man, "Hold your horses, Thorne! I'll handle this!" He turned to glare at Dorman again, "We ain't waitin' weeks! Where can we find him now!"

Dorman fidgeted, twisting in his chair and looking from one to the other of the men seated at the table. They were enough to make anyone nervous, and all leaned forward slightly to show their impatience. Dorman looked back to Foley, opened the flap on his leather satchel and withdrew a paper. He spread it out on the table and pointed, "This is town. Here is a road that leads to the farming community known as *Marais des Liards,* but locals call it Cottonwood Swamp. Now, about here," he pointed at the far end of the drawing, "is a farm with a sign overhanging the gate that says, *Haines.* He's been staying and working there, but he's in town often to visit with Auguste Choteau at the Trade Market."

"So, how far is it out to the farm?" asked a lean, hatchet faced man known as Leroy Hafen.

Dorman looked up at the one man that had sat

silent the entire time he was here, back to Foley and answered, "A little more than fifteen miles."

"How will we know him?" asked the fourth man, Chris Rice, who spoke more like an educated man with clarity and purpose. He was rather pleasant looking, clean-shaven, well-groomed, yet his attire was no better than the others.

Dorman answered, "He's about six foot, broad shouldered, has collar length dark blonde hair. Usually has a big black wolf with him."

The four men frowned, Leroy asked, "Wolf? Are you sure? Not just a big dog?"

"No, it's a wolf and a big one. And he's mean too, according to the one man that wasn't killed among those that tried to take him. He said the wolf tore the throat out of one of his friends."

The bounty hunters looked from one to the other, then to their leader, who growled, "Don't worry 'bout it. A lead ball can kill a wolf just as easy as a man!"

Dorman fidgeted again, "That is all I can tell you. Now, I must get back to work," and started to rise but was stopped by Foley's fist on his arm.

"What you told us better be right. If you're lyin', we know where you work. Don't forget that!"

Dorman leaned back away from the foul breath of Foley as he voiced his threats. As soon as he finished and removed his paw, Dorman stood, looked at each man and turned away to leave, hustling out of the place and quickly walking away, glancing over his shoulder, fearful he might be followed. The boardwalk was empty, and he slowed his pace, breathing deeply and shaking his head. He wasn't pleased with himself for his betrayal, but he was desperate for money. He was determined to return to real civilization in Philadelphia, he was tired of this backwater town and the disgusting people.

***

It was another sumptuous spread on the dining table this night, but there was something different. Although everyone was seated in the usual places, there seemed to be an undercurrent in the mood. Everyone was joyful and talkative and as Sophie served the deep-dish cherry pie, Elizabeth turned to Gabe and asked, "So, what did you think of the meal tonight, Gabe?" smiling broadly as she placed the linen napkin beside her plate.

Gabe looked at her and across the table to a smiling Eloise and Rupert, then back to Elizabeth, "Well, it was excellent, as always."

Elizabeth smiled even more, twisted around in her chair and gently laid her hand on Gabe's arm, "I'm so glad you liked it! You see, I cooked the entire meal just to show you I am quite capable in the kitchen."

Gabe frowned slightly, looked past Elizabeth to see a smiling Sophie nodding her head enthusiastically and adding, "Tha's right Mr. Gabe, suh. She done it all! Even the cherry pie!"

Gabe felt the heat rise on his neck, struggled to swallow, and looked at Elizabeth again, feeling a little like a mouse caught in a trap, and said, "Well, that's wonderful. But I never had any doubt that you could accomplish anything you set your mind to, and you've certainly done that!"

She clapped her hand gleefully, looking from Eloise to her brother and back to Gabe.

Gabe ducked his head slightly, lifted his eyes to Rupert and said, "But, not to change the subject, there's something I need to talk to all of you about."

"Oh, sounds serious and your expression says it is, so," started Rupert, glancing from Elizabeth to Eloise, knowing the women were expecting some sort of proposal.

Gabe glanced from one to another, saw their expectant expressions, then said, "Oh, no, it's not what you might expect. You see," and he placed his napkin alongside his plate, pushed the chair back and stood, one hand on the back of the chair, "I'm afraid I might have put you in danger." And he began to relate the events beginning with the duel in Philadelphia and the resulting bounty posted by the grieving and vindictive father.

"Normally, that would not be a problem. It's been a long time since that all happened and that was far away, but old man Wilson is worse than a snapping turtle and the last letter I received from my attorney told of the bounty being increased to $5,000.00. And the local banker has connections in Philadelphia and my attorney was concerned that Philip Dorman might have sent word as to my whereabouts."

"So, you think there might be bounty hunters coming to St. Louis to collect?" asked Elizabeth, aghast at the possibility.

"That is a definite possibility. And if Dorman was the source, he also knows I've been staying here."

"But, how soon are you leaving with Choteau's boat?" asked Eloise.

"That could be a couple weeks, maybe more," answered Gabe.

"Then, you'll just have to, how do they say, lay low!" declared Elizabeth.

Gabe grinned, chuckled, "When the bounty is that big, there's no telling how many, or when they will come. But, I don't want to endanger you folks, so, I was thinking about going into town, maybe staying at the St. Louis Exchange until time to go upriver."

Rupert stood, stepped behind Eloise, and said, "You are not just a worker on the farm, Gabe, you're our friend and the closest thing we have to family. You will stay here, but it might be best if you do as Elizabeth says," nodding to his sister, "and lay low. Maybe come in the back door, stay out of sight as much as possible, just to be safe."

"Well, I will have to go into town to meet with

Choteau at least once, maybe twice, more before we leave. Details, you know."

"I can go with you," offered Rupert.

"Or we can all go! Surely, they won't expect a group and they won't try anything with women present!" declared Elizabeth.

"That's kind of you to offer, ladies, but I will not put you in danger. Besides, we do not know the kind of men we'll be dealing with, it has been my experience that bounty hunters are not too concerned with whoever might get in their line of sight. All they see is dollar signs."

Rupert dropped his head, looked up to Gabe and suggested, "Why don't we all turn in for the night, and take things as they come. We don't even know if there are any bounty hunters, nor do we know if they'll arrive before Gabe leaves, so, let's just keep on with our lives as usual, maybe a little more cautious, but as usual as possible."

Gabe grinned, "Sounds like the best advice I've heard all day."

20 / Concerns

The slope below and the upper end of the meadows had been a beautiful palette of colors that held Gabe mesmerized in the fall. Now the hardwood trees had shed all their leaves and stretched skeletal limbs into the grey morning light. But he had been encouraged on his walk to his chosen place for his quiet time, when he saw buds on the branches, a sure sign of spring. The mornings were not layered with frost, the soil was giving way, and the time would soon be upon him to take to the river and return to the mountains. He smiled at the thought, then his attention was caught by timid footsteps coming through the trees. They were not the steps of a man on the hunt, but lighter, and confident. He caught a glimpse of the familiar form of Elizabeth and smiled as she appeared at the edge of the clearing that topped the little knoll and held the downed log that Gabe used as his seat and sometime altar where he spent his time with the Lord.

"Good morning," she stated, just loud enough for him to hear but not so loud as to startle the furry noisemakers of the morning. "May I join you?"

"Of course," answered Gabe, scooting toward the end of the log and motioning to her to have a seat.

"And to what do I owe the pleasure of your company?" asked Gabe, smiling and setting his Bible on the log beside him.

Elizabeth seated herself, twisting a little to find some comfort, then smiled at Gabe, "We are so seldom alone, and I wanted a little time for us to talk."

"Oh? I see. Am I in trouble for something?" he asked, grinning.

"No, of course not. But, since you spoke about the bounty hunters, this past week has made me do some serious thinking, and I thought I should clarify some things." She looked at Gabe, dropped her eyes and fidgeted a little, apparently trying to find the right words or the courage to say them. She looked up at him and began, "Gabe, as I think you have discerned, I have grown very fond of you." She saw him start to answer but she lifted a finger to stop him, then continued, "I've never felt this way about a man before, and it has confused me somewhat. I've thought about what I would like, and that is for you to stay with us and we become wed," again she saw him start to speak, but continued, "no, let me finish, please. But I know if that were to happen, you would never be truly happy and would probably feel more like a caged lion, and I could never have that. So, you're off the hook! Now that doesn't mean that I don't still have feelings for you, it's just that I understand and will expect nothing from you, except . . ." she paused to gather her thoughts, looked at Gabe to see his frown of question wrinkle his forehead, and she smiled.

"Every morning I've seen you leave the cabin and come up here to spend your time with the Lord. I know you read the Bible, pray, and sort out your day. But that day doesn't include me, and I realized I was jealous of your God, but I also came to know how ridiculous that thinking was and resolved to settle some things." She paused again, stood, walked around a moment and Gabe watched, waiting.

"As I've told you, I haven't been on too good of terms with the Almighty and you asked me what happened to cause that, and I never answered you, but now I want you to know." She walked around the log again, sat down, looked at him and began to explain about her youth and the time with her father and mother. "Although I was a toddler, my brother was older and our father promised, promised, mind you, that he would return after going off to fight in the war. But, of course, he never did. I spent my childhood trying to grow up as fast as I could because I watched my mother work herself to the bone and my brother become a man before his time. And all the while, my mother would pray, go to church, and wait for an answer to her prayers, but as far as I know, none ever came. So, I decided it was a waste of time to pray to a God that doesn't listen! But then you came along..." she glowered at him, trying to be angry but failing, ducking her head and staring at the ground, but a bit of a chuckle came as a slight smile split her face when she looked up at Gabe.

Gabe looked at her and asked, "So, because you didn't get what you wanted when you wanted it, you got mad and pouted all this time?"

She frowned at him, shook her head, "Well, when you put it that way, it does sound kind of silly, doesn't it?"

"Ummhmmm. So, do you know what your mother prayed for?"

"I assume for my father to return."

"Maybe, but maybe she just prayed for God's will to be done and for the grace to accept it, whatever that may be, and I'm reasonably certain she was like most mothers and prayed for her ornery kids to grow up to be responsible adults." He sat, hands on the log beside him, his shoulders hunched a little, then turned his face to her, "So, maybe her prayers were answered, you ever think of that? Oh sure, your father didn't come home, but perhaps God had another purpose for his life that was even greater, one that we'll never know till we get to glory and ask. Who knows, may-be he sacrificed his life and saved a whole bunch of others, or maybe just one that was destined for some special task in God's hand, but until we know, God gives us the faith to accept his will."

"But you talk like you know you're going to see Him someday, like you know you're going to Heaven. How can you know that for sure?"

Gabe smiled, "I was hoping you'd ask that. You see, Elizabeth, the Bible, God's Word, was given to us so that we *coul* know for sure that Heaven is our home," started Gabe, reaching for his Bible.

"But, after what I've done, the way I've talked about Christians, and other things. There is no way that I can get good enough or do enough to make up for what I've done, to deserve Heaven!" She shook her head, dropped her chin to her chest and stared at the ground.

Gabe saw a tear drop to the dust at her feet and said, "You don't have to, let me show you something," as he opened the Bible and scooted closer to her. He started with Ephesians 2:8-9 *For by grace are ye saved through faith; and that not of yourselves: it is the gift of God: not of works, lest any man should boast.*

"See Elizabeth, it says, 'not of works'. If it was based on what we do, the works, good or bad, then we would get the credit. But it's not! It is 'through faith.' And faith is just believing God." He paused, saw the light in her eyes and began going through the scriptures to explain to her the four things she needed to know. First, how we are all sinners, Romans 3:10 and that there is a penalty for that sin, which is death and hell forever, Romans 6:23. But God loved us so much that he sent His son to pay that penalty for us when Jesus died on the cross, Romans 5:8. And when He paid the price, He purchased for us the gift of eternal life, Romans 6:23b, a gift that all we have to do is receive by believing and asking in prayer, Romans 10:9-13.

"So, Elizabeth, do you understand these things as I've told you?"

"It's just that simple? All I have to do is believe in my heart and pray to ask for the gift?" she asked, eyebrows lifted, eyes wide, a smile on her face.

"That's all, but you must believe in your heart. This is not just some free ticket you get, just in case you need it," he cautioned.

"Oh, I believe!" she declared.

And Gabe led her in a simple prayer to ask forgiveness for her sin and for Jesus to come into her heart and life and save her from the penalty of sin and give her the gift of eternal life. When they finished, Gabe said, "Amen," and Elizabeth echoed that.

She looked up at Gabe, and said, "Is it all right if I give you a hug?"

Gabe grinned, chuckled, stood and held out open arms. Elizabeth stepped into the embrace and hugged Gabe with tears running down her face. She stepped back, looked up at him, smiling, "Thank you. I feel so much better." She turned away, said over her shoulder as she started to the path, "Come on, breakfast is probably waiting, and I can't wait to tell Eloise!"

It was a joyous breakfast, both Eloise and Sophie were especially jubilant with Eloise almost bouncing in her chair and Sophie singing and humming 'Amazing Grace' as she served the breakfast. She couldn't help herself and bent down to hug Elizabeth saying, "I'se so happy for you chile! Indeed I is! Ummhmm!"

As they finished their breakfast and pushed back from the table, Gabe announced, "I'll be going into town today. I need to meet with Choteau about the crew and cargo, is there anything I can pick up for you?" he asked, looking from one to the other.

Rupert said, "Are you sure that's safe? And don't you want me to go with you?"

Gabe shook his head, "We don't even know if there's anybody around, and I do need to meet with Choteau." He looked to Rupert, "It would be best for you to be here with the ladies, and I can manage on my own, and I'll have Wolf with me. It will be a quick trip and I should be back by dark." He turned to Sophie, "And I hope you'll keep supper warm for me, Sophie."

The big woman smiled broadly, "You knows I will, Mister Gabe, yessuh!"

***

The road to town was often narrow, hemmed in on

both sides by thick brush and trees, but in this time of early spring, the trees were naked, and the brush was thin, offering little cover. But the day was full of promise, the squirrels were scampering, looking for something fresh to eat, tired of their winter store of nuts. The swamps through the trees echoed with the clatter of ducks and a hawk let loose his rapid-fire caws as he circled overhead. In the road before him, Gabe grinned as he watched a bobwhite family stretch out behind their mother, each a mirror image of the hen with the exception of the furled topknot. It was a pleasant morning, but Gabe brought his attention back when he saw Wolf freeze in his attack stance and let the low rumbling growl of warning sound. He bent his head around to look at Gabe and with a quick hand signal from his friend, they took to the trees, going deeper in the woods to avoid detection.

Gabe quickly stepped down, bringing his rifle with him, as he hunkered down behind a gnarly cottonwood. Within moments, two scruffy looking riders came into view. They showed little concern and were talking to one another, mindless of their surroundings. The animals had gone silent, the only sound being the clatter of the horses' hooves on the hardened roadway, and the gruff voices of the two men.

"I'm tellin' ya, we don't need Foley! If'n we find that Stonecroft up here wit' these farmers, we take him. Put his head in a sack, go downriver an' catch us a boat and go back to Philly and get our money, all five thousand dollars of it!" The talker was a burly brute of a man, full whiskers, a floppy felt hat, ragged coat, with a rifle over the pommel of his saddle.

The second man, a thin rail of a man but attired much the same as his companion, squeaked his reply, "But if'n Foley finds out, he'll hunt us down and do like he did wit' that feller on the boat when he split him stem to stern with that big knife o' his! That might not skeer you, but I ain't intres'ted in gettin' turned inside out, nosirree!"

Gabe watched and listened, realizing these were bounty hunters, but the way they talked, there were more, but how many more? He watched them ride on as he thought. His dilemma was whether to confront them while there were just the two, and then what? Would it be safe for them to go to the farm? But the idea of allowing them to go to the farm and possibly endanger his friends didn't set well and made up his mind for him. He turned back to the buckskin, motioned to Wolf to lead the way, and rode back into the road, rifle over the pommel.

21 / Waylaid

Gabe had a thought, chuckled to himself and spoke to Wolf, "C'mon girl, let's have some fun!" He leaned down on the neck of the buckskin, dug his heels into the mare's ribs and hollered, "Heeeyawww!" They took off like the horse's legs were catapults outside an ancient castle and started on the road at a full gallop. He saw the two bounty hunters before him, and he shouted and screamed as the buckskin's hooves pounded a cadence on the hard surface. "Look out! Comin' through!" he shouted as he drew near, waving his rifle in the air over his head, "Thar's a bear! Big un!" he twisted around in his saddle, motioning behind him. He screamed as he plowed between the two, "It's a angry she-bear! She's a comin'! Ever man for hisself!"

The buckskin shouldered between the horses of the two startled men, who looked from Gabe to the road behind him, then to each other, and neither knowing what to do, leaned away from the man charging between them. But as Gabe went by hollering and screaming, waving his rifle, he smacked the bigger of the men, the one known as Jim Thorne, behind the head with the heavy barrel of the rifle, almost decapitating the man, unseating him and knocking him to the ground to land in a patch of briars, unconscious. The skinny man watched Gabe pass, frantically turned around in the saddle, then slapped legs to his hammer headed roan and took off in pursuit of Gabe.

"Wait fer me! Wait fer me!" he shouted.

Gabe looked over his shoulder, saw the first man unmoving in the brush, and started to rein up. He swung his horse around to face the oncoming bounty hunter that he would later learn was named Leroy Hafen, and stood in his stirrups, looking down the road as if watching for the bear. Leroy pulled alongside, "Whar's the bear? Is it comin'?" he shouted, twisting in his saddle to look back down the road.

Gabe slumped in his seat, took a deep breath and casually swung the rifle around to point the muzzle at the thin man. Leroy's eyes grew wide, he sucked in a breath and leaned back as if he could get away from the rifle. "Here! What'chu doin'? You said there was a b'ar comin'!" Then he looked down beside the buckskin to see the big black Wolf, staring at him, hackles raised. He looked up at Gabe, saw his eyes narrow, and started stuttering. "Uh, uh, uh, you're him, ain'tcha?

"That's right. Weren't no bear. Just me'n the wolf here. But 'fore we're done with you, you'll wish there was a grizzly bear."

"What'chu mean?" stammered the man, looking from Gabe to the Wolf, and back.

"You've got a choice. You can go back to the one you call Foley, you know, the one you're so afraid of that he might split you stem to stern with his big knife? Or, you can head on down this road, take that ferry across the river, and from there, well, just disappear."

"But, I ain't got no money! I cain't go nowheres without money!" he whined.

"Well, I could just shoot you right here, that way I'd not be worryin' 'bout you comin' back."

"You cain't do that!" he sniveled, looking like he was about to start crying. He was shaking and looking all around. He looked back to where his friend lay in the briars, saw his horse standing, reins trailing, and then munching on the sprigs of grass showing at the edge of the road. Gabe took a quick glance back at the man, saw him kicking, trying to free himself from the briars. He looked back at Leroy.

"Now, why can't I shoot you? That's what the two of you were gonna do to me? If I heard right, you were gonna shoot me, put my head in a bag, and go back to Philadelphia. Ain't that right?"

The man stared wide-eyed at Gabe, "You heard that?"

Gabe nodded, lifted the muzzle a bit to remind

him of his choices, then noticed the man look past
Gabe and start to smile. Gabe instantly dropped down
along the neck of the buckskin, heard the report of
the rifle from behind him, and slapped leather to the
mare as he heard the whiff of the bullet go past. With
two quick lunges, he was beyond Leroy, spun around
and one handed fired the rifle at Leroy as he was grabbing for his pistol. The big slug blossomed red at the
base of the man's neck, and the wide-eyed would be
bounty hunter fell sideways out of his saddle.

Gabe looked back to the first man, saw him scrambling to catch up his horse, and Gabe dug heels to the
buckskin. The bigger man had stepped into the stirrup
and started to swing aboard as the buckskin crashed into
the side of the roman-nosed bony bay of the scalawag,
and with the weight of the big man on the down side,
the horse stumbled, went down on his knee, fighting to
stay erect. Gabe saw the man snatching at his belt for
a weapon of some kind and Gabe plucked one of the
saddle pistols from the holster at the side of his pommel,
bringing it to full cock as he brought it up and dropped
the hammer of the double-shotted charge. The big pistol
bucked, spat smoke and lead, and the buckskin twitched
at the blast, but moved little. As the smoke thinned, Gabe
had brought the second hammer to full cock and he
leaned over to look at the man, but saw the body, with
nothing but a mass of blood and powder burn for a face,
crumpled at the edge of the road.

Gabe looked around, checking for any others, and satisfied there were no more, began reloading his weapons. As he worked, sitting astride the buckskin, he thought about what he had to do. There was no law man in town, although the leaders had been talking about finding someone, but there was an undertaker. He thought, *I reckon I better take 'em in to the planter and let him do his thing.*

As he rode into town, trailing two horses with bodies draped over the saddles, he saw several people stop and stare, but no one inquired or did more than take a long look. He reined up in front of the mortician's shop, tied off the horses, and stepped to the boardwalk. A man, attired in black, came from the doorway, and looked at Gabe, "Friends of your'n?"

Gabe shook his head. "Nope. Highwaymen. Tried to waylay me, but . . ."

"I see, and you want me to bury 'em?"

"That's right. I figure you can have whatever they have, horses, rifles, and such. That oughta be enough to plant 'em proper."

"Won't give 'em a marker," deduced the mortician.

"Don't know their names anyway," replied Gabe, as he went back to his horse, stepped up and swung his leg over. He nodded to the undertaker and gigged his horse to ride away. He was bound for Choteau's trading house and his meeting with the man.

***

When Foley sent Leroy Hafen and Jim Thorne to go to the farm and look for Stonecroft, he stationed Chris Rice near the trading house of Choteau and took up a lookout near the keelboat for himself. It was after mid-day and Rice walked to where Foley had stationed himself and asked, "We gonna go get somethin' to eat?"

"You hungry already?" growled Foley. He sat on the stone wall that separated the town from the riverbank and tossed a rock at the pile of driftwood that had stacked up at last high water.

"Yeah, and I could use a big mug of that ale, too," answered Rice. "Sides, we can see the street in front of the market and the wharf from the table in the Inn, so why not?"

Foley looked back at the corner window of the Inn, over his shoulder at the market and nodded, swung his legs over the wall and dropped beside his friend. They walked to the Inn and took the table in the corner as they waited for the Innkeeper to bring their food and drink. As they waited, they saw a man in buckskins rein up and step down. But they were watching for a city type, not a mountain man, trapper looking sort. They looked up as the innkeeper arrived with their meal, and gladly accepted the urns of ale.

***

Gabe had reverted to wearing his buckskins in the last few days, finding them more comfortable than the woolen trousers and linen shirts. With his hat tugged down to shield his eyes from the midday sun, his collar turned up to keep the cool spring air off his neck, he rode to the trading house, stepped down and tied off the buckskin. He motioned Wolf to stay and watched as he lay on the boardwalk in front of the mare. Gabe, rifle in arm, walked to the steps and in the door, squinting as he entered the dim interior.

He was greeted by Auguste, "Gabe! Good to see you. I was expecting you to drop in any day now. Glad you came."

22 / Meeting

The squeaking hinge on the door made Foley look up from his wooden bowl. He had been shoving the stew into his maw, taking little time to enjoy the meal, for he thought himself hungry enough to eat table, chairs, and all and had no time for savoring the makings of some Irishman that put anything and everything in the pot. A small man stood in the door, letting his eyes get used to the dim interior, apparently looking for someone. His breeches were too short, his jacket too tight, his head too big and his nose was too long. His rat face was accented with the absence of a chin and two snaggle teeth that pointed in opposite directions. When he saw Foley and Rice, he lifted his head, appeared to smile and toddled over to their table.

"Hehehe, you gemmen was wit' two other'n when you came into town, weren'tcha?" he squealed, sounding like a rat with his tail in a trap.

"What's it to ya?" growled Foley, glaring at the man over his bowl.

"Thot'chu might be int'rested in what 'appened to 'em," he squealed, putting his finger to the edge of the table to steady himself. He hobbled when he walked and was unsteady as he stood. He blinked often as he talked, "Fer a haf-dollar, I can show ye."

"Show us what?" mumbled Rice, sitting his empty bowl down and reaching for his ale.

"Wha' 'appened to 'em."

Foley scowled at Rice and then at the little man, "You'll tell us or I'll wring yore scrawny neck!" threatened Foley, reaching for the man's arm, but the wiry little man scampered out of reach.

"Ha'dollar!" he proclaimed, holding his hand out as he bounced from one foot to the other, his dirty face grinning as he cackled like a worn-out rooster.

Foley growled, dug into the pocket of his waistcoat, flipped a coin toward the man who watched it drop into the sawdust. The weasel quickly snatched it up, looked closely at it and grinned as he stuffed it into the pocket of his breeches.

"Hehehehe, I can take ye there, or show you the way!" he declared, waiting for a response.

"Where to?"

"The undertaker!"

"You mean they're dead?" asked Foley, surprised, "Both of 'em?"

"Hehehehe, better be! They's gonna get planted!"

"What happened to 'em?" asked Rice, unconcerned but interested.

"Hehehehe," cackled the little man as he bounced closer to the window, cackled again as he stood on one foot, the other at his knee, resembling a crane. He pointed out the window, turned toward the two at the table, "Hehehehe, him!"

Both men frowned, Foley rocking his chair back on the two back legs and stretching his arm to the window sill to keep from falling and looked out the window. A buckskin clad man was standing on the steps of the Choteau trading house talking to Auguste Choteau. Tied at the rail below the steps, the buckskin stood hipshot, head hanging and dozing.

Foley looked to Rice, back at the little man, "Him?" he asked incredulously. "That trapper fella in the buckskins?"

"Hehehehe," cackled the little man, bouncing from one foot to the other, "That's the one! Killed 'em both! Said they tried to waylay him so he kilt 'em!"

Foley slowly shook his head, anger boiling up within, and grabbed the now empty bowl and flung it across the room, bouncing it off the far wall, then dropped his fist to the table and banged it repeatedly, making it bounce and all the tableware rattle. The Innkeeper, standing behind the bar, lay a blunderbuss across the bar, cocked the hammer, "Here now! That'll be enough of that!" he declared, glaring at the two at the corner table.

Foley looked up, ready to charge, but quickly changed his mind at the sight of the blunderbuss, shook his head and nodded, lifting one hand in submission. He looked at Rice, "That sounds like sumpin' that stupid Thorne would do! Prob'ly figgered they'd take Stonecroft and collect the bounty their own selves. Well, that's what they get for tryin' to cut us out." He shook his head, leaned back to look out the window and dropped the chair back on four legs. He looked at Rice, "You ready to give it a go?"

Rice slowly grinned, nodded, "Two-way split? Of course!"

The two stood, then Foley led the way out. A quick glance showed the buckskinned trapper still talking to the other man on the steps, and Foley turned to Rice, "He don't know us, and we can take him by surprise. He's got him a rifle, but it's sheathed, you got your pistol?"

"Ummhmm," answered Rice, putting his hand to the pistol in his belt.

"And I've mine," replied Foley, also putting his hand on the butt of his weapon. He nodded across the street, "You cross up there, come down toward the horse from yonder like you was out for a stroll. I'll cross here an' come up on him. Wait till I get to him. If I can get him from behind, I'll just knock him out an' we can drag him below the wall yonder," nodding toward the retaining wall, "and finish the deed."

Rice nodded and started up the walk beside the brick building that housed the Inn. Foley waited a moment, then looking towards the river, ambled across the street, making it a point to not look in the direction of their prey.

***

"So, unless you have any additions to the bill of lading, we'll get started loading on the morrow!" declared Choteau, looking to Gabe for an answer.

Gabe's attention had been diverted when he saw the buckskin lift her head, ears forward and look at the end of the street. A lone man was crossing, coming from the Inn at the corner. But what made his skin prickle was when Wolf lifted his head from his niche between the hitch rail and the board walk and look up the street where another man was crossing. Both men were coming to the near side boardwalk, and both trying to appear nonchalant. But Gabe knew when people are behaving in a natural manner, they will look around. But these two seemed to make it a point not to look in his direction and also had their hands at their belt, probably on a pistol. Gabe frowned, stepped back from Choteau a half-step and turned slightly toward the street. He glanced at Choteau, "What was that?" he asked, glancing back to the men.

"I said, unless you have something to add, we'll

start loading tomorrow," repeated Choteau, frowning but not noticing what had caught Gabe's attention.

"Uh, sure," answered Gabe, and reached his hand into the sheath to bring the rifle to full cock, but keeping his action hidden with his body. He looked up at Auguste, nodded and watched the man turn back to re-enter the trading house. Gabe turned toward the street, holding the rifle across his waist, and casually took each step to the boardwalk. He paused, one foot on the last step, the other trailing behind on the next higher one, and looked from one of the men to the other, letting his eyes linger on the one coming from the river side. He glanced at Wolf, nodded and held his hand out, palm down, then brought it back to hold the fore stock of the rifle under the sheath.

Gabe acted like he was looking at something near the river yet watching the approach of the man from below. He was a sizeable figure, somewhat scruffy, and similar in appearance to the last two that confronted him, and Gabe quickly surmised they were together. As the man came close, he made a quick step, lifted his left hand and pointed up the street and shouted, "Look out!" expecting Gabe to turn away and look. But Gabe saw the man's hand move at his belt and knew he was going for a pistol, but he was too slow. Gabe thrust the rifle forward, catching Foley under the chin with the point of the butt plate on his rifle, jerking his head up and back and knocking him off the boardwalk.

Gabe looked to the other man, saw him bringing his pistol to bear, but the black shadow of the wolf rose from beside the boardwalk and the man flinched, just as Gabe dropped the hammer on the rifle, shooting from the hip and blowing out the end of the sheath. Smoke blossomed at the roar of the big gun, and the slug took Rice just over his belt, blowing through his innards and taking his backbone with it as it exited his body. Rice fell in a heap, and Gabe turned back to see Foley scrambling to his feet and grabbing at his pistol.

Gabe dropped the Ferguson as he pulled his over/under Bailes from his belt and lunged from the steps, stretched out in a leap to the dirt beside the steps, firing the pistol before he landed. He heard the bark of Foley's pistol, felt a tug at his sleeve, and looked to see Foley grab at his arm, bringing his hand back bloody. Foley glared at the man stretched out on the dirt, growled and clawed at his belt for his scabbarded knife.

Gabe rolled to his back and as he sat up, he pivoted the barrels to the unfired one, snapped it in place and cocked the second hammer. He lifted it toward Foley, "Don't do it!" he warned, but Foley snarled, "You can only shoot that thang oncet!" Foley lifted his knife and lunged toward Gabe, but Gabe squeezed the trigger, felt it fall, saw the flash of powder from the frizzen, but nothing happened. He glanced down quickly, realized it miss-fired, and tossed it away as he rolled to the side away from Foley's charge. He came to his feet quickly, tomahawk in one hand, knife in the other and stood in a crouch, looking at the man that wanted his head.

Foley snarled and glared at Gabe, "You ain't what we expected! But I'm gonna take yore head in a bucket back to Philly and collect my due!" and lunged, blade up. But Gabe tiptoed and sucked in his gut, making Foley miss and as Foley's arm stretched, Gabe brought his knife down and sliced his arm open, instantly drawing blood.

Foley jerked back, grabbed at his arm, glared at Gabe. "That was a lucky one, but yore luck's done run out!" He tried a sweeping cut, but again Gabe stepped back, making the man miss, but he followed up with a back swing and sliced off a section of fringe from Gabe's sleeve. As he stepped back, Gabe grinned, started pacing to the side, making the man circle, but Gabe knew he was stepping to the high ground, and watched the eyes of Foley, waiting for his charge. Foley had become wary, and watched his prey as they side-stepped, and as Gabe moved side to side, his moccasin turned a stone, and he slipped. Foley saw the misstep and lunged; knife held low. Gabe back stepped, stumbled and went down on his back. That was what the bounty hunter had expected and flung himself at the downed Gabe.

The massive form of the man was like an ominous thundercloud that bode no good will, but Gabe feigned fear, wide eyed, and as the man's feet left the ground, Gabe caught his bulk on the bottoms of his uplifted feet, grabbed his wrists and threw him over his head to land flat and hard on his back. Gabe quickly twisted around and came to his feet, looking down at the man who was gasping for breath and trying to get up. Gabe dropped to the ground, his knees beside the man's head and his knife at his throat, "Hold it!" ordered Gabe, and Foley went still. "Why are you tryin' to kill me?" Gabe knew why, but a crowd had gathered, and he wanted them to know what was happening.

"You know!" growled Foley, spitting blood.

"Tell me! Or I'll slit your throat ear to ear right now!" he demanded as he pressed the blade against his skin.

"The bounty! Wilson put five thousand on your head! Wants your head in a bucket!"

Gabe leaned back, lessened the pressure. "I'm gonna let you up now. If you know what's good for you, you'll leave this country and fast."

Gabe slowly stood, watched as Foley scrambled to his feet and knew he still had his knife. Gabe knew what to expect but hoped the man would make a better choice. Gabe dropped his eyes and started to turn away, showing the bounty hunter his back, but a sudden gasp from the crowd made Gabe drop to one knee as he twisted around, just in time to see Wolf come from beside the buckskin and catch the man's arm in mid strike as he was starting to throw the knife into Gabe's back, but the hundred and sixty pounds of wilderness wolf knocked him to the ground and a woman screamed as Wolf tore at the man's arm.

"Wolf, no!"

The big black wolf stood astraddle of Foley, blood dripping from his jowls, turned to look at Gabel and at the signal, went to the side of his friend, leaving a wimpering, bleeding Foley grabbing at his arm, pulling it to his chest.

The knife lay out of reach and Choteau stepped forward and picked it up. He tossed a rag at the man, "Bind up your arm and get out of this town and be gone before dark. If anyone sees your face again, I'll have the entire town after you!" He watched as the big man stood, put one end of the long binding in his mouth and with his free hand, wrap it around his arm repeatedly, then tie it off. He glowered at Choteau and Gabe and stomped away.

Choteau walked to Gabe, "I see what you mean when you say there might be bounty hunters about."

Gabe chuckled, "I hope he's the last. Four in one day gets a little tiresome."

"Four?!"

"Ummhmmm." He nodded to the body on the boardwalk beyond the horses, "and I dropped off their two partners on my way into town."

Choteau looked at Gabe, shook his head, grinned. "I reckon we better get that boat loaded and get you outta town!"

"Suits me!" answered Gabe as he picked up his rifle, examined the sheath, shook his head and started to mount up. He nodded to Choteau, reined the buckskin around, motioned to Wolf, and started out of town.

23 / Lading

It was the cold nose of Wolf that brought Gabe instantly awake. But the big black wolf still lay quiet beside him, watching him open his eyes and stir to wakefulness, no alarm, no growl, just his friend waking him. Gabe smiled, rolled to his side and ran his fingers through the scruff at Wolf's neck, "Mornin' boy! Been a while since we woke up together in the woods. You got breakfast on the fire yet?" He chuckled as wolf scooted closer, wagging his tail like a widow woman's broom, and smiling at his friend. "Well, you ain't no more anxious to get goin' than I am!"

It was the first grey light that spread its skirts across the eastern sky, reflecting the muted color in the rippling waters of the mischievous Missouri River as it bid good morning to the rising pair. Gabe rolled from his blankets, stood, stretched and looked to the buckskin. Standing beside the mare was a big bay mule,

Gabe had traded the strawberry roan back to Rupert for the big mule having been told by Rupert how much more dependable the jack would be on the trail. He was also broke to ride and could spell the buckskin when needed. Although the animal wasn't too friendly with Wolf, he knew that would come in time.

Gabe wasted little time gearing up, he had put the pot with last night's coffee on the remaining coals, and quickly downed it, put the pot in the pack on the mule, and was soon on the trail to town. They had spent the night in the woods just northwest of town and the orange fingers of the rising sun illumined the roadway as he entered the sleepy village. He made his way to the riverfront, went to the wharf where the keelboat sat and noted the hubbub of activity as the men finished loading the boat. Choteau stood on the wharf, writing board in hand, as he checked off the lading as each bundle or package was lifted aboard. He looked up to see Gabe, lifted a hand in greeting, "Mornin'!" he declared and looked at the next bundle.

Gabe tethered the animals, motioned Wolf to stay with them, and mounted the wharf to walk to the side of Choteau. He nodded to the remaining boxes and bundles, "Looks like that stack is 'bout finished!"

Choteau looked up, "Ummhmm. Mebbe another quarter hour or so." He pointed to the stern of the boat, "There's a boarding plank yonder for you to load your animals. There's already some hay and grain on board, but you'll need to feed 'em on shore as much as possible."

Gabe nodded, "Figgered that. You want me to load 'em now, or later?"

Choteau looked up from his bill of lading, "Maybe now would be best. That way they can get used to the boat before it starts moving. Don't want 'em getting spooked and raising a ruckus."

Gabe nodded, went to the stern and began manhandling the loading plank. It was a heavy plank about thirty inches wide with several cleats to give the animals footing. He lifted the end, stepped to the wharf and secured the plank. He walked across it for a test, and satisfied, went to retrieve the animals. He led the buckskin aboard without incident, stripped off the saddle and dropped it in the corner of the corral nearest the cabin. The rear of the cabin had a single door in the middle, and the rear wall served as the one side of the corral. When Gabe brought the mule up, the long-eared beast hesitated, dropped his head for a closer look, lifted to look at the waiting buckskin, and without any encouragement trotted across the plank into the small corral beside the horse. Gabe grinned, chuckled as he shook his head, then replaced the plank behind the rear of the corral. He stood in the stern, looked at the slow-moving water of the mighty Mississippi, and wondered just what he was doing aboard a keelboat when he should be high in the Rocky Mountains with Ezra. He grinned, shook his head and turned, thinking, *Soon, soon.*

He walked the *passe avant* or running board at the side of the boat to the forward end of the cabin where the gangplank stretched to the wharf. Choteau came aboard and motioned Gabe to follow. They ducked through the door to enter the cabin. Both men ducked their heads as they looked at the stacks of goods. Choteau started reading the lading, "600 pairs of blankets from one-half point to three and one-half points, 300 bolts of fabric, 100 dozen mirrors, 100 dozen knives, 600 scalping knives, 50 trade fusils, 50 dozen combs, 100 gross buttons, 3000 pounds blue and white beads, 600 half axes, 300 tomahawks, 30 American felling axes, 20 battle axes, 500 pounds vermillion, 150 pounds verdigris, 12 gross clay pipes, 3000 pounds gunpowder, 3000 pounds of lead and 4000 pounds tobacco, and 300 copper pots." He looked from his lading to Gabe, "Think that'll do?"

Gabe chuckled, "You're the trader, but as far as I know, that should be enough for the entire Assiniboine, Hidatsa, and Crow nation, and probably the Gros Ventre as well." He turned to leave, noticed a stack nearer the door, frowned, "And that?" he asked, motioning to the stack.

Choteau grinned, "*That* is the most important, at least for the crew. That is the food and such that will make the journey more pleasant on everyone. There are several cases of rum as well. A crew of mostly Creole from the New Orleans area have need of their proper sustenance.

But they're good men, as you'll find out."

"Oh, I'm sure they are, after all, they are men of your choosing, are they not?"

"Most of 'em, some were brought on by the Patron, Galvez or the Bosseman, Duplessis. Most came upriver with the boats, but I believe there's a good crew."

Gabe frowned, "Boats? I thought this was the only one."

"No, I had two. One is at the boatyard being outfitted for other trading ventures. I plan on bringing more loads from Pittsburgh, stoves and such are in great demand here and in St. Genevieve, and whiskey from Pennsylvania as well. All with a goodly profit," declared Choteau as they stepped back to the wharf.

Choteau turned to Gabe, "There are twenty-three crew. The Patron, the Bosseman, the midshipman, and twenty polemen. You will not be expected to do anything aboard the boat, so enjoy your journey on the water. Once you go ashore, then your responsibility will be to provide ample meat for that hungry crew," he stated, nodding toward the crew that had started boarding with their warbags, "and of course, guiding them through Indian territory." He paused, looked up to Gabe, "Once they have decided on a location for the post, your duties are done. And as you requested, I'll bank your shares under the Haines account."

Gabe reached out to shake Choteau's hand, "I'm certain this will be a profitable venture for us both. And if

I'm needed, leave word with any of the posts or any of the leaders of the tribes, and I'll do the same." Choteau nodded, smiled and the men shook hands and parted, Choteau to his trading house and Gabe to the boat.

***

Most of the men were on board when Gabe stepped back on the boat. He walked back to the stern, preferring the company of Wolf and his horse and mule. He upended a bucket beside the fence, leaned back against the boards, and looked to the river. Behind the boat, there were two pirogues, the smaller craft would sometimes be used to help tow the keelboat in deep water. The men were busy about getting ready to put out to the water, twelve had taken their place on the benches in the prow and were readying the long oars. Others were busy racking *les perches* or the poles that would be used when poling the boat. Two men stood side by side, aligning the poles atop the cabin when one elbowed the other just as Gabe made his way along the running board on the far side of the boat. The first man, Xavier Roche, said, "Remember what that man Foley said about the fella they were after?"

The second man, Valentin Marcon, asked, "What fella?"

"You know, the one that had that five-thou-sand-dollar bounty on him."

"Oh, yeah. What of it?"

"He said the man's name was Stonecroft, and he was tall with blonde hair."

"Yeah, so?"

Roche pointed with his chin as he handled a long pole, "Look at him, that's the one what's gonna be our guide. Look at his hair."

Marcon looked up, watched Gabe take his seat behind the corral fence, then back at his friend, "Looks kinda brown to me."

"Yeah, well, I heard the Patron refer to him as Stone."

Marcon frowned, looked at his smaller friend, "Mebbe. But I thought them other fellas were gonna get him sure."

"Mebbe they couldn't find him, or mebbe he got them first."

"So, what good does that do us?"

"Look, that fella Foley was braggin' that night they got into the rum, that all they had to do was get that Stonecroft's head in a bucket or sack, take it back to Philadelphia and collect the reward." He paused, made a quick glance in the direction of the stern where Gabe was seated, "So, if'n that's him, and Foley and his friends failed, then what's to stop us from collectin'? Five thousand's a lotta money!"

"Yeah, but we don't know if that's him, and even if it is, he don't look too easy to take," cautioned Marcon.

"We'll just bide our time, mebbe get to know him, you know, ask some questions, watch what he does.

Shouldn't be too hard. Two of us, only one of him."
Marcon chuckled, "Ummhmm, there were four of
Foley's bunch."

Roche frowned, looked to the poles, "Uh, yeah."

***

"A bas les avirons! Shouted the Patron for the rowers to
drop the oars into the water. He ordered them to push
at the oars to back the boat away from the shore, then
the order was for the starboard side to raise their oars,
and the port to dig deep. With the Patron at the rudder, within a few moments, the keelboat had turned
into the current, although staying close to the west
bank of the Mississippi. As they hit the confluence
current where the Missouri dumped into the Mississippi, the Patron steered them into the Missouri, and
they were on their way.

Gabe watched the Mississippi recede from view,
slowly disappearing as the Missouri bent west and
south to straighten out to the northwest. The Patron
had ordered the other eight crewmen to raise the
mast, and Gabe glanced over his shoulder to see the
men atop the cabin, struggling to raise the mast, insert
the four large hardwood pins, then lash the mast with
wide rawhide straps. Once secured, at the order of the
Patron, they unfurled the sail, about a hundred sixty
square feet of canvas. When the wind caught the sail

and filled it out, the Patron hollered, *"Levez les avirons!"* And the men at the oars lifted them from the water, stood them on end then dropped them between the benches and the running boards.

As the boat moved steadily against the current, the quiet of the river settled over the boat and Gabe saw the south west bank and knew the Haines farm was just out of sight. He remembered the conversations of the night before when he said his good byes to the family, the well wishes that were given and the hugs all around. And when Elizabeth followed him out onto the veranda, they talked a while longer, sharing thoughts about what might have been and what could be still if he chose to return. "Elizabeth, if for a moment I considered leaving the mountains, this would be the first place I would choose to come, here, to you. But, well, it's hard to explain. That country gets into your blood, your spirit, and you become a part of it, and it becomes a part of you. I feel I am just as much a part of that wilderness as the grizzly bears, the elk, the mountain sheep, even the sunrise and sunsets. To see the snowcapped peaks painted with the colors of the rising sun, well, there's just no other sensation like it, and every sunrise is different and awe inspiring. I could never leave it again, and I wouldn't want to, not ever."

Elizabeth dropped her head, spoke softly, "If it was another woman, I'd fight for you and never give up until you were mine. But I can't fight the entire western world! I wish I could know the west like you do, see the mountains, the native people. But know this, I will never see another sunrise or sunset that I don't remember you."

Gabe looked down at her, drew her close and they embraced, holding to each other tightly. But Gabe had to pull away, and turn away, for it is hard for a man that has any empathy in his soul at all, to look upon a woman who was sincerely grieving at a loss, and not be moved. He stepped to the buckskin, swung aboard, and with a simple motion to the wolf and the lead rope of the mule in his hand, he swung the buckskin around and started off. He turned to look back one time, branding his memory with the image of this woman, and this place, something he would treasure always.

24 / Exploring

By the end of the third day out of St. Louis, Gabe had seen the crew work at moving the boat in more ways than he cared to consider. The sail helped for about a half day until the morning breeze out of the east died down, then the crew started poling. With ten men on each side, they would line up with the long ash poles with the end that looked like a shoe and the other with a knob, put the knob into the hollow of their shoulder, the shoe in the water and would literally walk the boat upriver by pushing against the stationary pole and walking along the running board. Then they would lift the poles, walk back to the prow end and do it all over again. But when they came to the bend that carried the deep current the water was too deep for the poles and the men had to go to shore with the long line, about eight hundred feet long, and cordelle or pull the boat. The end of the line was bound to the base of the mast, threaded through the bridle ring that kept the towline above the water and at the prow of the boat, and twenty men on shore would line out and pull the boat along.

Gabe was most impressed by the work of Etienne Duplessis, the Bosseman, who was easily the biggest man aboard, and would stand at the prow, use a pole to keep the boat off the bank, but most importantly, would watch the river for obstructions such as rocks, sandbars, or snags, anything that could hinder or damage the boat. Whenever he spotted an obstruction, whether a rock or sawyer, a partially submerged tree that had been swept into the river by some flood, or an embarrass, which was a floating mass of uprooted trees, dead animals, or other flotsam, he would shout out, direct the cordelle crew and/or the Patron at the rudder, and coordinate the efforts of all to bypass the obstruction and save the keelboat any damage.

The men worked daylight to dark, with few breaks or rests, but Gabe was continually amazed, for when they came aboard for the evening meal, they would chow down and once finished, the music would begin and the singing, dancing and shouting would go on into the night. But the men would be roused at first light, and the day would be repeated.

As the sun was rushing toward the western horizon, Gabe had geared up his mounts, and once the boat was tied off, he stretched out the planks and went

ashore. He needed to feel the solid ground beneath his
feet, and he thought Wolf would appreciate a good
run in the woods. Dusk had always proven to be a
fruitful time for hunting, and he was wanting some
fresh meat, already tired of the sow belly and beans
that had become the staple. He also knew this was
the border land between the Osage and the Nutachi
native peoples and he wanted to see if there were
any villages nearby. Although both tribes had proven
friendly to white men and especially traders, Gabe
preferred to be as knowledgeable as possible.

Once on solid ground, Gabe stretched, stepped
into the stirrup and gigged the buckskin into the
trees. Wolf leaped ahead and took to a game trail as
if it were the path home. Gabe grinned as he followed.
The shadows were already growing long, and two
squirrels high up in a tall oak, scolded the passersby,
but were soon left behind. When the boat had moored
in a slight cove on the south bank, Gabe had spotted
a break in the trees about a mile upstream that he
guessed to be the mouth of a small feeder creek and
it was that creek they were bound for, hoping to find
some deer coming for their evening drink.

The trees thinned out as the trail neared the creek.
It was a shallow valley that carried the narrow stream
from the low hills south of the river. As he came to
the edge of the trees, Gabe reined up and stepped
down, slipping the Mongol bow case from beneath

the left fender of the saddle. He sat down on a nearby log, used his feet to string the bow, and stood, bow in hand as he hung the quiver at his belt. He had tethered the horse and mule, and with Wolf at his side, started from the trees, but had gone just a few steps when Wolf froze in place, head down, hackle raised as he stared toward the willows at Creekside.

Gabe dropped to one knee beside Wolf, nocking an arrow as he knelt, looking at the line of willows, searching for the cause of Wolf's concern. On the far side, back in the trees, stood several tipis, and people were busy about the camp, but no one was near the creek nor close enough to have spotted Gabe and Wolf. Gabe touched Wolf on his shoulder and slowly moved back into the trees. Once under better cover, Gabe searched the village for any indication of who they were, although he was certain they were Osage, since this was their territory, but also because the Osage were an easily identifiable people. The men were tall, muscular and shaved much of their heads, leaving a scalplock that trailed down their back. The women wore their hair long and straight, yet their attire was similar to many tribes, the decorations the only difference between them.

Gabe watched intently, trying to determine if they were just on a spring camp or hunt, or if it was for a raid or something else. But the people seemed busy with the usual affairs of a camp that was supportive of a hunting party. Nothing looked prohibitive and Gabe decided to make himself known. He replaced the arrow in the quiver, stood, and with Wolf at his side, started toward the camp.

He had crossed the creek and was walking up the low bank before he was spotted, but the warning sounded quickly and the women quickly gathered the playing children to their sides, and several warriors stepped to the edge of the camp, most armed with rifles or bows, and watched as Gabe approached. He raised his free hand, palm forward, and spoke in Osage, the language he learned his first winter in the territory when he stayed with the Osage people, "Greetings! I am a friend!" he declared, stopping and keeping Wolf at his side.

Gabe saw the reaction of the warriors as they looked from him to Wolf and back, but one man stepped forward, "You speak our language. What are you called?"

"I am Spirit Bear, but known as Gabriel, a friend of the Osage. I spent one winter with the village of Blue Corn and Eagle's Wing," answered Gabe.

The warriors looked from one to the other and back to Gabe. "I am White Raven. I am the leader of this village. My woman has spoken of a white man named Gabriel; she was of the village of Blue Corn." He turned and called back to the village for his woman to come forward. When the woman parted the men and stepped forward, she stopped and stared, then looked from White Raven to Gabe and back, then ran to Gabe and threw her arms around his neck to hug him tightly as she said, "I thought I would never see you again!"

Gabe pushed her back to look at her, and as he recognized her a smile split his face, "Amomakwa! Honey Bear!" and hugged her again. They stepped apart and an obviously embarrassed Honey Bear, eyes dropped to the ground, spoke softly as she pointed back to the warriors, "This is my man, White Raven!"

White Raven had come forward when his woman ran to this man and now stood frowning, as he looked from Gabe to Bear. He grinned as he looked back to Gabe, "My woman has spoken of you before. She said you were a good friend to her and the people of her village."

"And they were friends to me. Had it not been for Honey Bear and Eagle's Wing, I would probably have crossed over a long time ago," explained Gabe, but he remembered the time spent with her and her people fondly. It had been a very memorable and pleasant winter, their first in the wild territory.

Raven and Bear both looked down at Wolf, then back at Gabe and Raven suggested he come with them into the village. "Woman, make us some food for we have a visitor."

Bear trotted ahead to their lodge to finish her preparations for the meal while Gabe and Raven walked together. Raven asked, "What has you in our land?"

"I am traveling on a boat from the trader Choteau.

I return to the Rocky Mountains where I have made my home."

Raven nodded, understanding, "We have traded with Choteau. He is a fair man."

"We just stopped for the night; we'll push on in the morning. It will take us the passage of three moons before we get to where we're bound. Both men knew Gabe meant the full cycle of the moon, or what whites referred to as a month.

"It is a long journey. What people are there?"

Gabe chuckled, "We pass through the lands of many different people. Ponca, Omaha, Mandan, Arikara, Assiniboine, Crow, Gros Ventre and more."

Raven stopped and frowned as he looked at this white man, "You have been among all these people?"

Gabe chuckled, "And more. I took a woman from the Shoshone, made friends with the Arapaho, Bannock, Salish, fought the Crow and the Blackfoot, made friends with some as well."

The evening was spent over good food and even better conversation. Both men spoke of learning from one another, and Gabe shared what he had learned about the far country. When he lifted the grizzly necklace from under his tunic, both Raven and Bear marveled at the claws and listened intently as Gabe told of such massive bruins. It was obvious that Raven and Bear were happy together and Gabe told of his time with Pale Otter and told of her making the necklace for him. "I am called Spirit Bear among her people, but I was given the name by the Arapaho." He reached into his possibles pouch and withdrew the other necklace to show and pointed out the pale fur at the base of the claws, "That is the fur of the spirit bear in the far northern mountains. It is for this bear I am named."

***

When Gabe rode back to the camp by the boat, it was just before first light and the glow of their cook fire showed the men had rolled their blankets in the trees, preferring solid land to the rocking boat. He had the carcass of a big doe across the pack of the mule and as he circumvented the camp to reach the campfire, he tethered the animals in the trees and slipped the carcass to the ground. The midshipman, Nigel Morgan, the only non-Creole of the bunch, did double duty as the cook and when Gabe stepped into the light of the rekindled cook fire, Nigel was wide-eyed and smiling at the sight of fresh meat.

"Ah, me boy! Sure'n tis a sight for sore eyes to see some fresh meat for a change!"

"A change? We've only been on the river for three, goin' on four days! And you're the cook!" declared Gabe, grinning and laughing at the man.

"Aye, what you say is true, but tis a welcome change, no less!" he declared as he sharpened his carving knife on the steel.

25 / Upriver

Gabe stripped the two deer carcasses from the mule, dropped them on the ground and led the animals off to rub them down. It had been a week since he met with the Osage and he had spent most of that time in the woods, riding ahead of the boat, scouting the area for possible threats, as they were nearing the land of the Kansa. Although they had been friendly with the whites, Gabe was well aware of what a band of renegades could do before anyone was ready to defend the boat. He had alternated from the north to the south shores, scouting and hunting.

He rubbed down the buckskin with a handful of dry grass, picketed her on some fresh graze and went to the mule to give him his due. Once finished, he stacked his gear beneath a big elm tree, then walked back to start skinning the two deer. The two had been hung from a big branch of a sprawling oak and one man was already at work skinning one out.

Gabe grabbed his smaller knife from the scabbard at his back and started on the second carcass. He glanced at the other man just as he spoke, "So, it's Stone, isn't it?" he asked.

"Ummhmm," answered Gabe, sliding the blade smoothly between the flesh and hide. He stuck the blade into the tree branch and grabbed the hide to pull it down from the rump of the deer. When it became difficult, he used the knife again, trimming close to the flesh. The hides would be kept and used for trading, giving the women of the tribes the opportunity to tan and prepare the hides for their use or trading as finished buckskin.

"So, what gets a fella like you to leave home an' become a scout?" asked the man, then added, "Oh, I'm Xavier Roché, I come from N'O'lns like the rest o' the crew. Didn't have nuthin' back there, joined up with a boat crew 'n been pushing wood ever since. How 'bout you?" he added.

"Oh, just wanted to see the territory an' the mountains," surmised Gabe, pulling at the hide again.

"Where you come from?" asked Roché.

Gabe frowned, looked over at the man, "Somethin' you need to know about this part of the country. It can get almighty dangerous to start askin' questions of any man. Most folks that leave what they call civilization, do so for their own reasons, and most don't want to share those reasons. I've known of men to get their heads split open just for askin' questions."

"Oh. Live an' learn, huh? Does that apply to you too? I mean by my askin' questions?" he probed.

Gabe finished pulling the hide down the carcass, cut away around the neck and dropped the hide to the ground. He looked at the man, scowling. It appeared as no more than a flick of the wrist, but the bloody knife tumbled through the air and impaled itself in the haunch of the deer within inches of the man's face. Roché's eyes flared, and he looked back at Gabe as he walked closer. Gabe reached up and plucked the knife from the carcass, and glowered at the man, "Oops!" he said. Then wiped the blade on the hair of the deer, turned his back on the man and walked away.

Roché let out a deep breath, what he had been holding since the knife stuck in the carcass and watched Gabe leave. He grinned, finished his work and left. He went to the moored boat, caught the eye of his friend, Valentin Marcon, and motioned him to join him in the trees. The trees, though thick, were just budding out and still appeared as skeletal apparitions of winter, but the thick brush also provided cover as the two men walked close to the shore, upstream of where the boat was moored.

"I talked to him! And I'm certain he's the one Foley and the others were after!" declared a grinning Roché.

"What'd he say?" asked Valentin.

"When I asked why he was out here, he said he just wanted to see the Rocky Mountains! And that's what

Foley said 'bout the man, that he left Philadelphia to go to the mountains!"

"But, how d'we know its him? Stonecroft, I mean?"

"When I asked him where he came from, he got real upset. Threw a knife at me, he did!" sniveled Roché, picking up a stone and chucking it into the river.

"Threw a knife? An' didn't hit'chu?"

"He wasn't tryin' to hit me, just warn me to mind muh own business." He groveled, kicked at a stick, then looked back at Valentin. "That man's dangerous. I think he got Foley 'fore he an' his men had a chance!"

"Then what are we gonna do? Foley had more men!"

"Yeah, but he don't know we're after him. We can take him when he's asleep, slit his throat, take his head, and be gone 'fore anyone knows it!"

Valentin grunted, "You make it sound easy, but I don't think so."

The men sat down on the grassy bank and Roché began, "Look, I been watchin' him. He comes back to camp most ever' night but rolls his blankets away from the rest. He stays with his horse an' mule and that wolf. But I've seen that wolf go to the woods come dark, mebbe he's huntin' a pack or sumpin' to eat, but he don't always stay close."

Valentin grinned, squirmed around a little to face his friend, and asked, "So, you're thinkin' we can watch for when the wolf leaves, then sneak o'er an' take 'im?"

"Yup, just like that. We can move through the

woods quiet like, one on either side, an' first one goes for his throat, the other'n hold him down."

"Sounds easy 'nuff, but, I don't know. I'm gonna hafta think on it a spell," mumbled Valentin. Although he was the bigger of the two, he was a little slow in his thinking and wanted to consider things carefully. He had gotten in trouble all too often by just acting on impulse or when he had too much to drink. This job with the trader offered an opportunity to get his life straightened out, maybe go back to New Orleans with some money saved, and if Gabrielle was still willing, they could get married and have a home.

He tossed a stick into the water as the two sat quietly, then thought about the bounty. Five thousand dollars, and he would have half. That was more money than he would have if he stayed with the boat and trader and he could be back in New Orleans by the end of the year. He grinned at the image of the waiting Gabrielle, hoped she still waited. Then looked to his friend, "We'll do it."

"Good, good. Now, we just have to wait till it looks right. You know, the wolf gone, his camp away from the rest, and when it looks good. But, we've got to be doin' it soon. Go too much further, it'll be hard goin' gettin' back to St. Louis."

"We gonna take one o' them pirogues?" asked Valentin.

"That'd be the best way, don'tchu think? It's too far to walk an' I ain't int'rested in meetin' up wit' any them Indians!"

"Me neither," mumbled the big man.

***

Nigel Morgan had put on a sumptuous meal of venison stew with wild turnips, onions, and meat. He had whipped up biscuits and potato cakes and finished it off with the last of the spring rhubarb, made into pies. It was the pattern to cook enough for the next day's meals at the same fire, and just warm things up on the stove on the boat. When the men had pushed back from their tins and mugs, the designated cleanup crew went to work at water's edge, while Nigel cut strip steaks and hung them over the hot coals. The fresh meat would be the following day's meal and easily prepared onboard.

Gabe had his fill and started for his blankets when the Patron, Phillipe Galvez called to him. Gabe turned, saw the man motioning him to join him and went to his side. Galvez bid him be seated, and Gabe sat, accepting the offered cup of coffee, took a sip and looked to the man.

Galvez looked toward the others who were moving about, probably getting ready for some music and more, then looked to Gabe. "You've been doing a good job getting fresh meat, just like Choteau said you would, and I be thanking you," he began, but paused, looked again toward the others then back at Gabe.

"Now, I usually don't inquire into the backgrounds of men that work with me, but I overheard something that concerns me, and maybe you too."

"Oh, and what was that?" asked Gabe, sipping his coffee as he leaned forward, elbows on his knees.

"I did not hear enough to make sense of it, but I first heard it before we got to St. Louis. There were four men that caught the boat in Pittsburgh, worked on the crew from there, but they were never friendly with the others. They kept to themselves, but I did hear something about a bounty and someone they were after." He paused, looked to Gabe with raised eyebrows as if waiting for a response from his scout. But Gabe remained silent, listening attentively.

"I didn't think much of it, they did their work and the only trouble they were was when the crew got into the rum, that's when I heard the talk. But the men got off and did not want to stay with the crew and were replaced by crew from the other boat of Choteau. Then I heard it again, two men were talking as they put away the poles, probably didn't think I could hear, but all I heard was the word, 'bounty.'" He paused and looked to Gabe again.

He continued, "I was at Choteau's trading house when you came to see him. I also saw the shooting outside." Again he paused, giving Gabe an opportunity to speak. "Those men were two of the men that came from Pittsburgh on my boat."

Gabe looked at the Patron, "And the men you heard talking onboard were not of the original four from Pittsburgh?"

"No, they were not. I do not know these men; they were referred to me by a friend in New Orleans and I trust my friend. But I have not gotten to know these two, although they are good crewmen and have been no trouble. They have done nothing to be disciplined for, and just talking is not a crime. But, I thought you might want to know, just in case."

Gabe looked at the Patron, then dropped his eyes to his cup, took the last swig and tossed the dregs aside. He looked back to the man, "Thanks. I'll be on guard." He started to leave, then paused and turned back to the man, "Just so you know, the bounty is not a legal one, it's a grudge from an evil man that wants vengeance when vengeance is not warranted."

"I thought so. I have too much confidence in Choteau to think he would have a man as his partner that was less than reputable."

Gabe nodded, turned away to return to his separate camp and tend to his animals. Wolf lay near his blankets and Gabe dropped to his knee beside him, ran his hand through his scruff, "Boy, we're gonna hafta be watchful. There's more bounty hunters around somewhere."

26 / Practice

For several days the Missouri River had borne to the
northwest, but on this day it made a pair of bends
and eventually bore to the southwest. The banks were
well forested, and few landmarks shown above the
treetops. The banks showed little variety with mature
hardwoods hanging heavy branches low over the water, making it difficult to cordelle. The Patron sent
four men with heavy axes ahead to clear the brush
and limbs where possible, but it was impossible for
the men to fight the heavy branches and they had to
resort to warping, where the rope crew had to go to
the length of the rope, tie it off, and the men on board
would walk the rope in, pulling the boat along. Some
keelboats had availed themselves of a winch appara-
tus, but the space for a winch was loaded with cargo
and the men had to hand-over-hand the rope aboard,
stretch it out again and repeat.

A small cove just before the confluence with another smaller river offered cover for the coming night and the Patron steered the boat into the bank, called out the orders to tie off the hawsers, and the boat was made fast. The routine of offloading provisions and bedrolls was quickly undertaken, and the tired men stretched out for some rest before the meal. Gabe had traveled on the boat this day and now offloaded his animals, picketed them on some graze and was starting toward the camp when he saw movement in the trees. He slipped the Ferguson from the scabbard and dropped to one knee to look below the low-hanging branches of the riverbank.

Approaching the camp was a small group of natives, about four or five best he could make out through the trees. He watched them come, slowly sidestepping toward the camp and paralleling their course. As they drew closer, he saw they were carrying hides and pelts, and didn't see any carrying arms as if to attack. Gabe whistled to catch the attention of the Patron, saw him turn, and with a nod, motioned to the approaching Indians.

Gabe stepped into the clearing of the camp, holding his rifle across his chest, but ready. He recognized the shaved heads with the small scalplock and knew they were Nutachi, or Missouri people, allies of the Jiwere, or Otoe, and known to be friendly. As they neared, the leader held up an open hand, called "Aho! We trade, whiskey."

The Patron motioned them closer, motioned for them to be seated on the log, and the leader and one other seated themselves, as the other three stood behind them. All held pelts and hides and were looking around at the men and the camp. Gabe stood stoically, watching them, trying to determine if this was a genuine trade mission or a scout before a raid.

Phillipe, the Patron, and trader, said, "Let me see," motioning to the pelts. He looked closely at each one, feeling the fur of the pelts, examining the smoothness of the hides, going from one to the other, keeping each stack separate. When he finished, he asked, "What do you want to trade for?" using sign language to make himself understood.

"Whiskey! We want whiskey!"

"Is that all, just whiskey?" asked Phillipe. "I'm not supposed to give you more than two jugs of whiskey. Would you like some beads or knives?"

The men looked from one to another, speaking in their tongue which Gabe recognized as a dialect of the Siouan, similar to what he knew of the Osage. He understood enough to know they were arguing about whiskey or knives and one asked about a tomahawk. The leader turned back to Phillipe, motioned to the stacks of pelts, said, "This many," holding up four fingers, "whiskey. This many," holding up five fingers, "knives and one tomahawk."

Phillipe shook his head, "Two whiskey, five knives, two tomahawks."

The warriors looked to one another, arguing, gesturing, then the leader turned again, "Two whiskey, five knives, four tomahawks."

Phillipe looked hard at the man, slowly shook his head, then extended his arm and the men clasped forearms, sealing the deal. Phillipe turned to Etienne, "Get 'em their stuff."

When Etienne returned, his arms were loaded, and he dropped the knives and hawks, then handed the jugs of whiskey to Phillipe. The trader in turn passed the jugs to the leader who grinned, looked to his friends, and jumped up to leave, almost forgetting the knives and tomahawks. But the others grabbed up the rest, and the five trotted off into the trees.

Phillipe looked to Gabe, nodded and grinned, "It was good to have you standing there with that rifle. I noticed they kept looking at you as they dickered. Wish I coulda understood what they were saying, but we made a good trade."

"They were just arguing about the goods. I was watching because it is a common tactic to send someone in to trade, just to scout out the camp." He motioned around, "I know you told the men to always have their rifles and kit ready, but if you look, you'll see there's only a couple that have 'em. If that had been a scout, they would have told the others this camp would be easy to take because no one is armed and ready to fight."

"I'll have a talk with 'em," answered Phillipe.

Gabe shook his head, "Do you know if any of 'em can shoot? I mean hit anything when they do?"

"No, I'm not even sure they know how to load a rifle. We're used to traveling the river, not the wilderness."

"River pirates?" asked Gabe, surprised the Patron and his crew had not had to fight off pirates.

"There's some on the Ohio, not too many on the Mississippi. Guess we just got lazy."

"If you have to defend this boat against some renegades that don't want to trade, thinking it would be easier just to kill everyone and take what they want, then you might wish you had been better prepared."

"Do you really think there are those that would do that?" asked Phillipe, disbelieving.

Gabe shook his head, "Any band can have renegades, and I've come across some, including some renegade French traders from one of the big companies, that wouldn't have to even think about it before they'd try to take this boat. There's only twenty-five men, and at any time, the most you could have under arms is half that, the others would be tryin' to handle the boat. Any of the tribes along this river could put together a raiding band of fifty to a hundred warriors within an hours' time. And everyone of them wanting to earn honors by killing an enemy and taking his scalp and all the bounty aboard this boat." Gabe shook his head and walked off into the trees to check on his animals, wondering all the while what he was doing traveling with these pilgrims.

***

Choteau had outfitted the crew with a modified Pennsylvania rifle, .45 caliber, made by the Dickert Rifle works. Similar to the 1792 Army Contract rifle, it had a barrel of only forty-two inches, and was easily handled aboard the boat with the close quarters. The rifles had been issued to each crew member along with the necessary accouterments, possibles bag with balls, mold and tools. Come morning, the Patron called the men together after their morning coffee and biscuits, "Men, we need to get more familiar with our weapons. Those Indians that came walkin' into camp yestiddy, well, we can't be lettin' that happen. So, I've asked our scout, Gabe, to help with you men and your shootin'."

He looked to Gabe, motioned him forward, "We're just gonna do the basics, cleanin', loadin', and shootin'. So, if you will gather up your weapons, we're goin' to that clearin' yonder and get started."

There was some grumbling, but several also saw it as a break from the tedious and tiring work of the cordelle and more. They gathered in a bunch at the edge of the trees and Gabe stood before them, looking them over, noting how they handled their rifles. Several stood with rifles at their side, butts on the ground and muzzles close. Others had lain them on the ground and dropped to sit beside them, some were seated with rifles across their laps, and one used his as a crutch, with the muzzle to the ground and the butt under his shoulder.

"First off, you need to know this might be the only thing that saves your lives. When there's fifty screaming warriors attacking, your shot might be the one that kills the warrior that's intent on taking your scalp." He paused, breathed deep, marshalling his resolve and patience when a man called out, "Whatchu mean take my scalp."

Several of the men looked at the questioner, the same man that had used his rifle as a crutch and stood grinning. Gabe looked at the man, walked closer, and suddenly used the butt stock of his rifle to knock the crutch from under the man, and with his heel behind the man's calf, pulled him to the ground. Gabe dropped with one knee on the man's chest and with his rifle barrel across the man's throat, he quickly slipped his knife from the sheath between his shoulder blades, and brought it to the man's hairline, one hand holding the man by his hair and the blade just above the man's eyes. Gabe growled, "Scalping is when the warrior uses his knife, and cuts around your skull like this," he lightly ran the tip around the man's skull, "and jerks your hair," Gabe snatched at the man's hair enough to make him yelp, "and takes it off, hangs it from his belt, and if you're still alive, he'll slit your throat from ear to ear, and while you're bleeding out, he'll cut off your genitals and maybe your hands and your feet. All while you're still conscious and bleeding out. The last thing you'll see is the blade of that warrior with your blood dripping from it!"

Gabe pretended to wipe the blood from his blade, slipped it back in its sheath, grabbed his rifle and stood. He offered his hand to the man who was shaking and had wet himself, but the man rolled over and crawled away. Gabe watched as the fleeing man went behind the others, then looked at the rest of the men. "Now, as I was saying. Your rifle might be the only thing that keeps your hair on, so you need to keep it clean. If you fire it four or five times, it could become so fouled with powder residue, it won't shoot properly or at all."

He continued into the late morning, teaching them about the weapon, cleaning, loading and finally gave each man an opportunity to shoot at a distant target. Of the twenty crew men, four hit the target, several came close, and two, including the original question-er, missed by at least the length of the rifle, which prompted Gabe to give a quick lesson about using the rifle as a war club. By the end of the morning, the men were confident they could defend themselves, but Gabe not as much.

"Patron, at least they know how to load and pull the trigger. That's more than some knew this morning. But, if you have a choice to stand and fight or take to the water and run, you might prefer the water."

"That's encouraging. But do you really think we'll need to fight?" he asked.

Gabe shook his head, "I've been among many tribes and one thing is certain, and that's there is no way you can predict what some chief will decide, or some war leader choose to do, or even a band of renegades might try." He looked at the Patron, "Most of the native people will only make an attempt against an enemy if they're certain of victory. If they think they will suffer too many losses, they won't do it. Maybe if you maintain a show of arms, well, then again," he paused thinking.

"What?" asked Phillipe.

"If the natives see so many rifles, they'll also be tempted to take them, but if they see enough to know we're armed and can and will use them, then they'll consider more carefully."

"Yes, I see what you mean. We have included some trade fusils, but not very many. Choteau said the natives were always asking about trading for guns, but he didn't want to do that, afraid they would use them against us."

"And they would, but they are a very valuable trade item, maybe a better gift item for the chiefs or other leaders," suggested Gabe.

"Well, at least I feel a little better about the crew." The Patron lifted his eyes to the sun, shading them with his hand at his brow, "We can still make some miles, so, we'll be getting underway soon. Will you stay aboard, or take to the woods?"

Gabe grinned, "After that little demonstration, I don't think I made too many friends aboard. I'll take my chances with the natives and the animals."

27 / Plot

For three days, Gabe stayed on shore, scouting and hunting, coming to the boatmen's camp of an evening with the day's take of meat. He was at home in the woods, even though the forests of the lowlands were different than the pine woods of the mountains. Here the trees were thicker and now that summer was coming on, the trees were leafing out, everything greening up, it was almost claustrophobic for a mountain man. But he trusted Wolf and the buckskin to find trails where none appeared to be and his sense of direction seldom wavered, for a man of the wilderness depended on the position of the sun, the direction of the shadows, and more.

But by the dawn of the third day since his shooting school, Gabe found himself on the edge of a wide basin of grassland, dotted by clusters of trees and swales that held low growing thick brush. He sat in his saddle at the tree line, looking out across the open space, an openness he had not seen for some time. He watched as white tail deer scampered about, new born fawns gamboling with abandon, their mothers watchful, and yearlings showing buds where antlers would grow, staying to the side by themselves. Gabe heard some movement off to his left at the edge of the trees and spotted two black bear cubs racing up the side of a towering tulip tree with their mama rolling rocks at the base, looking for grubs.

About forty yards beyond the bear, a shadow moved, and Gabe leaned forward to look, then stood in his stirrups, grinning as he slowly sat back. He reached for his rifle and swung his leg over the rump of the buckskin to drop to the ground. He turned back to a cluster of trees, tethered the horse and mule on long leads so they could graze, and with Wolf at his side, ducked into the trees to start his stalk.

With all the greenery, ground cover was damp, and limp, and he moved silently through the trees. In a short while, he started toward the tree line, gauging his distance and position by the tree tops. As he drew near, he dropped to one knee, listening. He grinned as he heard the rattling bellow made by the buffalo bulls as they moved and grazed. They were the biggest animals in the country and had few predators, except man and sometimes cougars, and they were afraid of nothing, so when they moved, it was not with stealth. Gabe listened a moment, then started to move closer. As he neared the tree line, he saw the shadowy form of the big brown woolies and carefully took a position beside a big elm. He was about fifty yards from his chosen target, a young bull that grazed close to a cow and her calf.

Gabe slowly brought up his rifle as he leaned against the tree trunk, saw the big herd bull that was nearer the edge of the small herd, lift his head and look his way. But Gabe knew their eyesight was not particularly good, yet he froze in place, not even breathing. He waited until the bull dropped his head and resumed his grazing. Gabe breathed easy, bringing the hammer on the Ferguson to full cock, slipped his finger to the small forward trigger, and narrowed his sight. Placing the front blade on the low chest, just behind the front leg, he took a breath, let some out, and squeezed off his shot. The Ferguson roared and spat smoke and lead, the herd bull jerked like he had been poked and lifted his head to look directly at Gabe. The big lead ball punctured the rib cage of the young bull, blossomed red, and the bull took two steps, lowered his head so his beard touched the ground, struggled to take another step, and dropped on his chest, rolling slowly to the side.

Gabe had his eyes on the herd bull, knowing that the big beast could run faster and farther than he could and with those horns could hook him and throw him high over his back for he had seen it happen. But this bull did not take a step, and with no other movement from the trees, he sauntered off to the far edge of the broad meadow, looking for more fresh shoots of grass for graze.

Gabe breathed easier, dropped the butt of his rifle beside his foot and set about reloading. Once done, he returned to the horse and mule, stepped aboard, and went to the carcass to start the hard job of field dressing the big beast. Wolf was at his side and when they came close, Wolf was first to the beast and started sniffing around, cautiously at first, then growling and snapping until Gabe stepped down and went to work. But Wolf was committed to doing his part and as Gabe tossed scraps and entrails his way, he savored the task and bent to it with all his might.

***

Although still in the land of the Nutachi, or Missouri people, the river was due to make the bend to the north at the confluence with the Kansas river, and the land on the west bank would be that of the Kansa or Kaw, a people known as fierce fighters and not as friendly with the traders, although Choteau had established a post at the confluence, and done well trading with them. At least until the new Spanish governor allowed only his own picks to have the licenses and all others were disallowed, causing Choteau to leave his post and return to St. Louis.

Gabe was on the north shore and had agreed with the Patron that they would make camp on that side, or as the river bent to the north, on the east bank, and it was on the east bank just upstream from the confluence with the Kansas River that the boat put in for the night. The river made a sweeping bend around a point of land at the confluence, then pointed to the north. On the east bank, a break in the trees showed a low bank of grass and sand, an alluvial deposit from eons of floodwaters pushing the effluence into the bend. They tied up to a big oak and stretched out the gangplank and at the direction of the Patron, the planks for boarding the horse and mule. Gabe had said he wanted to board the boat and offload across the river. Although he could make it across, the animals would be swimming in deep water and against a strong current and would be tired out quickly, so he chose to use the boat so they could spend the time on shore.

The men had the unusual treat of sitting on the bank and watching the setting sun put on its spectacular show of colors as it sent lances of gold and orange across the western sky. Once it dropped below the horizon, the colors, though a little muted, were like a patchwork quilt lain over the canopy of the sky. Even the men, hardened by merciless and seemingly endless work, little appreciation for their labors, and no recognition, appreciated the display of colors by the Creator.

They lined up for the evening meal and were just finishing up when Gabe dragged into the camp, mule and horse both loaded with the de-boned meat of the bison, wrapped in the pieces of hide strapped to the pack saddle on the mule, and behind the saddle of the buckskin. Wolf flopped on his belly, watching Gabe swing down and stand beside the horse, grinning at the cook, Nigel, and the Patron, Phillipe. "Got you some buffalo! Best meat there is! But you gotta get somebody else to unload and cut it up, I'm beat!"

"Buffalo! Ah dinnae ken 'boot dat! I heerd it to be mighty braw, so we be seein' to it, aye!" declared Nigel, motioning to the designated helpers for the evening. They quickly unburdened the animals while Gabe grabbed a tin of stew, sat, and made short work of it. He led the animals to the trees, found an isolated spot at the base of a big oak, and dropped his saddle and gear beside it. He led the animals to the nearby grass, picketed them and rubbed them down. When he went back to his gear, Wolf had already stretched out, rolled to his back, and was snoozing with all four feet in the air. Gabe chuckled, rolled out his blankets, and set to cleaning his rifle. He reloaded it, checked the loads in his belt pistol, fluffed up his jacket for a pillow and as he stretched out on the blankets, he reached up to ensure the saddle pistols were within reach. He lay back, hands under his head, and looked past his feet to the stars that lit their lanterns in the west, remembering the day. He usually had help when he took a buffalo, for among the natives, it is the work of the women to dress out the big beasts. But alone, he had to skin it, use the buckskin to roll it, and finish skinning. Then disemboweling it was a smelly, bloody task, but the deboning of the thousand-pound animal was the most demanding job. He was thankful it was over, and tomorrow he would show Nigel how to prepare the Depuyer.

He listened to the sounds of the night. At river's edge, bullfrogs were tuning up for their evening choir. The rattling call of a kingfisher seemed to say goodnight and the ever-present owl asked his question of the night. In the distance he heard the deep throated howl of a loon.

He breathed deep, reliving the day, and knew he was more tired than usual. He seldom dropped into a deep sleep, easily stirred to any change in the night sounds, and he trusted Wolf and the buckskin and mule. He slipped the belt pistol to lay it beside his head, his hand nearby and rolled to his side, facing the animals, and relaxed. Tired as he was, he was soon fell asleep.

***

"Come on!" whispered Roché, pushing against the shoulder of his friend and co-conspirator, Valentin Marcon.

"Whuh?" mumbled the big man, looking through squinted eyes at the source of his disturbance.

"Now's the time! We can do it tonight!" whispered the excited Roché, looking around at the other sleeping forms. They had purposely put their blankets at the edge of the grassy bank and away from the others, but he was concerned that one of those might stir and see them on the move. "Come on," he urged and crawled back from the man.

Valentin rolled from his blankets, reached under his gear bag for his knife and pistol, but Xavier shook his head as he pointed at the pistol, "No, that'll wake everybody!" he whispered hoarsely. "Just the knife." Roché turned away and crawled to the trees. Once under cover he stopped, came to his knees and waited for Valentin to come close. "I saw the wolf go to the trees, and he told the cook he was tired out, so he'll be sleeping sound. We won't have a better chance."

Valentin looked at him, "I don't know, are you sure?"

"Yes, c'mon," he mumbled and turned to lead the way in a round about route to come from the thicker tree cover toward the sleeping form of the scout. When they were within about ten yards, they stopped, and in a low whisper, "You come from behind that tree, low down, crawl if you have to, but quiet." He nodded to the opposite side, "I'll come from there. When you see me move, you come! I'll go for his throat, you hold him down, lay on him if you have to!"

Valentin nodded and started for the far tree. When he moved away, Roché started for the big tree that would be his starting point. They were anxious, yet moved quietly through the underbrush, getting as close as possible. The scout lay beneath a big tree, his head by the base of the tree, and the black wolf was nowhere to be seen.

***

As Gabe had dropped off to sleep, he stirred, the hackles on his neck raised, and he looked into the darkness. But there was nothing moving, the night sounds had not changed, and he rolled to his back, dropped his hand to Wolf's neck, and with a simple motion, sent the wolf into the trees. He rolled back, eyes wide, looking at the horse and mule, but they stood hipshot, heads down, snoozing. Gabe breathed easy but listening to the night. A flutter in the trees told of a nighthawk leaving his perch, but it was a flight of alarm. The only sounds now were the distant croak of the bullfrogs. Even the loon had gone silent. He glanced at the buckskin who now stood, head up, ears pricked. He was looking to the trees beyond and behind the mule, then turned to look past Gabe to the other tree line.

Gabe slipped his hand around the grip of the pistol, slowly brought it to full cock, muffling the sound with his blanket, and waited. The whisper of cloth against the brush told of the approach of one from the brush and trees before him, and the soft crunch of a boot sole on sand told of a second attacker. He took a slow breath, waited, then when the rush of feet sounded, he rolled and came to his knees, leveling the pistol at the first attacker and dropped the hammer. The blast of the pistol shattered the stillness of the night as it spat flame and death. The impact of the bullet stopped Roché as he grabbed at his chest, rose up on his toes, and fell forward, dropping the knife under him.

Gabe spun around, spinning the barrels on the pistol and cocking the second hammer, to see the bigger Valentin rise from his crawl and start to charge, but Gabe hollered, "Stop!" and the big man, eyes wide, mouth open, and arms flung wide kept coming. Gabe dropped the second hammer, but his aim was low, and the bullet took the man in the side, spinning him around and dropping him to his knees. Valentin grabbed at his side, turned his head to look at Gabe, eyes pleading for mercy, as Gabe reached down to snatch up one of the saddle pistols, cocking it as he lifted it level. He stepped toward the big man, "What are you doing?" he asked.

"It was his idea, he wanted to get the bounty," grunted Valentin, wincing at the pain in his side.

The Patron and several of the men had come running at the first gunshot and now heard Valentin try to explain. "Help me, I'm dying," pleaded the big man.

The Patron motioned to Nigel, who was known to be the best at doctoring, and the man trotted off to get the necessary bandages. Phillipe stepped beside

Valentin, "Are you saying that Roché and you were goin' to kill Stone here, for a bounty?"

Valentin nodded his head. "It was all his idea, he said it would be easy. But I tried to talk him out of it," moaned the big man, trying to move his legs from under him.

Phillipe looked at Gabe as Gabe lowered the pistol, then looked at the crumpled form of Roché. He shook his head, looked up at Gabe, "What should we do with this one?"

Gabe shook his head, "Patch him up. You need every hand and I don't think he'll try it again."

Phillipe looked at the others that had gathered, then back to Gabe, "What about them? They heard him say 'bounty' and they'll be asking about it?"

Gabe grinned, "After that," nodding to the body, "and that," nodding toward Valentin, "do you think they'll try?"

Phillipe grinned, "Not if they're smart, but nobody ever accused a crew member of a keelboat of being smart."

Gabe shook his head, sat down on his blankets and started reloading his belt pistol, returning the saddle pistol to its holster. Wolf lay beside the blankets, having returned at the first gunshot, and would have taken Valentin, but Gabe shot him first, so Wolf just lay down and waited. Gabe ran his fingers through the scruff of his neck, "What took you so long? That big guy mighta had me!" then chuckled as he rubbed behind the wolf's ears. Maybe now they could both get some sleep.

28 / Otoe

The fog lay heavy and thick, treetops stretching above the mists like islands in the clouds. It was quiet, and what few sounds there were had been muffled by the blanket of willowy whiteness. Gabe sat beside his small hat-sized fire, watching his coffee pot dance on the rock, wondering about the day that lay before him. He had walked through the wispy ground-hugging cloud, moving his hands as if he could push it away, as he walked mindlessly but in prayer and thought. Now he sat beside the fire, feeling his solitary isolation. He lifted his eyes, could see only as far as the shadowy forms of his horse and mule, reached down to run his fingers through the scruff of Wolf's neck, "Well boy, this pea soup sure makes us feel like we're all alone in the world, but maybe it'll burn off soon 'nuff."

He reached for the pot, poured some thick black brew, savored the aroma as it rose from the steaming cup, and nibbled on the last of his biscuits. He had put some smoked meat in the fold of the biscuit, both had absorbed the heat from the flat rock, and now he enjoyed this tidbit for his breakfast. He saddled up, loaded his gear, and by the time he was on his way, the sun was doing a number on the fog.

It was mid-morning when movement in a swale stopped him. He reined up beside a cluster of trees, watched the slowly dissipating fog as it parted for the movement beyond. Moving to the west was a caravan of people and animals, natives on the move. He reached back to his saddlebags and retrieved his telescope, stretched it out and searched the bottoms. Directly before him stood the round huts of the Kaw village, a few people still working at their morning tasks, but the majority of the villagers were on the move, probably headed to the prairie lands of the west in anticipation of the great migratory herds of buffalo. These people, like most of the other tribes of the natives, were dependent on the buffalo for most everything they needed. Usually they would have a spring hunt, and if necessary, a fall hunt. The hides of the buffalo provided the lodges, the meat their sustenance, and every other part was used in one manner or another, bones for tools, scrapers and such, tendons for thread, innards for containers, and all manner of things.

As he looked at the village, he noted there were mostly old people, some women and youngsters, and a few young men left behind to hunt and protect the others. The village was well back from the Missouri and totally concealed from any passerby on the river or the trails that followed the water. These were the Kansa or Kaw people, and this was a small village by their standards, probably thirty huts. It would not be a profitable stop for the boat, so he resolved to circumvent the village, and work his way back closer to the river.

***

The next morning saw a clear sky and lifted spirits. Even the buckskin and mule seemed to step lightly, Wolf was playful, and Gabe was smiling as they followed the well-traveled game trail through the trees. The boat had been well supplied with meat and he had no need of bringing in game, at least until the end of this day, so he was watchful for any meat on the hoof, just in case. The terrain was of low rolling plains, thickly forested for the most part, but some areas of open meadowland that soaked up the morning sun and brought blossoms to the wildflower patches, making for a colorful passing.

The river made a wide bend to the west, then back again to the north, the land changing little, but with every rise or open vista, Gabe would stop and search the land for any sign of villages or other passerby. They were nearing the land of the Jiwere, or Otoe, allies of the Nutachi, or Missouria. By late afternoon, Gabe crested a slight rise that had a bald knob and he stepped down, tethering the animals in the shade, and went to the crest with his scope. Below him and nearer the river lay a sizable village, and he began a slow scan.

As he watched, he saw a gathering, perhaps a council of leaders, outside one of the larger mud-hut lodges. He recognized the shaved heads with mohawk style roaches or scalp locks, and knew they were the Nutachi. The others had full heads of hair, cape like tunics, and scalp lock braids that dangled over one shoulder. These would be the Jiwere. He saw several dugout canoe pulled up on the bank at river's edge, undoubtedly from the Nutachi or Missouria band. But it also looked like there was more activity than what would be expected, and Gabe surmised they too were getting ready for their spring buffalo hunt.

He looked back along the river, caught a glimpse of the keelboat, and guessed they would be abreast of the village soon. Calculating the distance and the time, he had to decide whether to go to the boat or go to the village to set up a trade, he chose the trade. He stood and returned to his animals and started to the village.

***

It did not appear to be a warm welcome as eight warriors stepped forward, several with nocked arrows in their bows, others with lances and war shields, two with trade fusils, all with stern expressions. Gabe reined up, lifted one hand in the recognized sign for peace, and said, "Aho! I come in peace, to trade." He had dropped the reins to the neck of the buckskin and used both hands to sign, keeping his hands away from any of his weapons.

One formidable looking man, one of the two with rifles, stepped forward and spoke in Niúachi dialect of the Siouan language, also sign, "You are not welcome. Leave!" with a swift motion of his hand and turning slightly away.

"It is for your leaders to decide. I have many coming on a big boat," motioning to the river, "with much trade goods to make trade with both the Nutachi and the Jiwere," replied Gabe, making no move to leave.

The leader turned back, scowling at Gabe, then looked at one of his men and barked an order with a quick motion that sent the man running into the village. Within moments, an entourage of people came from the interior of the village, led by two impressive looking figures easily identifiable as one Nutachi and one Jiwere. The taller of the two with a roach that added to his mohawk hairstyle, stepped slightly forward, and spoke, "You wish to trade, but you have little to trade!" motioning to the packs aboard the mule.

"There is a large boat coming up the river with much trade goods. Whiskey, beads, knives, cloth, and more," answered Gabe.

"You have whiskey?" asked the leader.

"Yes, and more."

"Who are you?"

"I am Spirit Bear from the far away mountains, but the trader is from Choteau. He is called Phillipe."

The men looked from one to another, Gabe guessed because they recognized the name of Choteau, and the leader looked back at Gabe. "I am Big Horse, leader of the Nutachi. This," motioning to the man beside him, "is Little Thief, leader of the Jiwere. We will trade. When will your trader be here?"

Gabe looked to the sun, back to the chief, "Before the sun sets, but they will probably want to trade after first light in the morning."

"This is good. We will trade," declared Big Horse, turning away and leading the group back to the interior of the village.

The leader of the warriors stood his place, scowled at Gabe, and motioned him to go around the village to the river. They stood unmoving as Gabe reined the buckskin away, and started toward the river, but it was then that Wolf came from the brush to follow, and the warriors jumped back as the big black wolf trotted beside the buckskin, keeping the horse between him and the warriors. The men chattered among themselves, gesturing toward the wolf and the man that led him away, but they stayed where they were until Gabe disappeared into the trees.

Gabe rode along the bank of the river, looking for a likely campsite and tie-off for the boat, and found one just downstream from the opening at the tree line where the many dugouts rested. He stepped down, walked the area, and satisfied, picked the site for his own camp and tethered the animals, stripped the gear and had no sooner dropped the saddle beside a tree, than he heard the sounds of the approaching boat and went to the riverbank to flag them down.

***

It was a profitable trade, resulting in several bundles of pelts and hides, a lessening of the load of trade goods, but leaving the trader with ample supplies for his trade post, wherever he chose to establish one. They pushed away from the bank just after mid-day and were soon on their way upriver. Gabe had left early, not wanting to involve himself in the trades and anxious to put some miles behind him.

They were nearing the land of the Omaha and Gabe remembered friends they had with the Omaha people and wondered if he might find them. It would be good to see them again; they were a special people and they had shared some good times. He smiled at the remembrance of the woman Running Fox and her family that included her grandfather, the chief of all the Omaha. If they could meet again, it too would be a profitable trade.

He stopped for his mid-day meal and breather for the animals, now tethered at the edge of some trees while he sat in the shade of a big sycamore. He dug some Depuyer from his saddlebags, remembering Nigel's response to the unusual substance taken from the backbone of the bison. When Gabe explained the dense fatty substance, and that he had to deep fry it in hot grease for about thirty seconds then smoke it for most of a day, he responded, "Awa' an bile yer heid!" which Gabe suspected that Nigel thought he was joshing him, but he reassured him and the man did as directed, but when he told of the need to smoke it, he said, "Yer bum's oot the windae!" and Gabe rightly judged that to mean Nigel thought he was daft.

But after it was finished and Nigel had a taste, he was duly impressed and when Gabe explained it would last indefinitely, he nodded, took another tidbit, and answered, "Guid gear comes in sma' bulk!" meaning good things come in small packages. Gabe grinned, took a good portion, and went to his camp.

Now he was glad he did and also glad that Nigel had agreed to keep the secret of such goodness between the two of them. With a nod and a wink they sealed the deal and Gabe knew the big cut of Depuyer would be a treat enjoyed for some time.

29 / Recognition

When he lay his head back to look at the stars, he caught a glimpse of earth born night lights. It had been some time since he had seen the dance of the lightning bugs, and he sat up to enjoy it. He was camped close to river's edge, thick grass carpeted the bank, and it was from this moist greenery that the light show arose. He was taken back to the time of his youth when he and Ezra would camp out in the woods and watch the dance of the night fairies on wing. And like most youngsters, they chased after them, seldom catching one, but always marveled when they opened their fist for a close-up look at the blinking lights of the bugs.

He lay back, cradling his head in his hands, and thought about his friend and his wife, and possibly first child by now, wondering where he might find them. But there was still a long stretch of muddy river to travel before he came to a jumping off place where he could leave the trader and his vassals and goods behind and cut across the plains to the high mountains. He knew the Rockies did not have these fairies of the night, but the close-up look at the stars far exceeded any display of these winged creatures.

***

He was glad to be on the trail again, leaving the land of the Kaw, Otoe, and Missouria. He chuckled at the remembrance of the two chiefs, Big Horse and Little Thief, and their demands for more whiskey and their perturbance at Phillipe's refusal to provide more. The leaders of the Otoe and Missouria had apparently developed quite a taste for the devil's brew by the many trades with the French and Spaniards. But Choteau had his limits and Phillipe held to them, giving only four jugs to be shared among the chiefs and whoever they chose. The chiefs had risen from the trade blankets, mumbling and threatening, but they didn't stop the trades. Now the boat was passing through the land of the Iowa and bound for the land of the Omaha, Ponca, and others.

As Gabe remembered his time with the Omaha and Ponca, a smile split his face as he rocked in the saddle to the gait of the buckskin, thinking about Running Fox and her people. Between the Omaha and the Ponca, the two tribes controlled all the trade along the river, allowing only those they knew to bring goods and trade with their people. They also restricted the area from other tribes, like the Pawnee and others.

His subconscious was stirred to attention when he saw several turkey buzzards circling high up and back from the river. He saw a small knoll, pointed the buckskin that way and when he crested, he reined up and stepped down, slipping his scope from the saddlebags. A wide field spread below, dry, showing only the blue grey of gramma grass with tufts of bunch grass interspersed with mounds with prairie dog lookouts perched atop each one. He searched the broad expanse until he saw the still form of a downed horse and stretched out nearby a young warrior. He watched for a short time, and the young man did not move, perhaps he was injured, or even dead. As Gabe looked things over, he put together the tale of the flats. The man had been riding through the prairie dog village, either pre-occupied with something or fleeing something, and his horse had stepped in a hole, broke his leg and thrown the young man. But the horse was dead, either from a broken neck, or mercifully killed by the young man. He watched for a short while longer, glanced up at the turkey buzzards, saw a pair of coyotes stalking the potential meal, and stood, went back to the buckskin, and swung aboard.

As he rode into the dry grass field, the coyotes slinked away, but the turkey buzzards continued their circular flight. Gabe drew near the downed horse, saw the leg bent askew, then looked to the still form of the young warrior. He too had a broken leg, the bone protruding from the skin below his knee. Dried blood had caked beside the break, and the sign in the dirt showed the young man had tried to drag himself away, but he lay still. As Gabe looked, he saw the warrior's chest rise slightly, but his eyes did not open. His color was pale and his eyes sunken, Gabe knew the young man had lost a lot of blood, and based on the sign, had been here since late the day before.

Gabe stepped down, ground tied the buckskin and mule, reached into the packs, and pulled out a bundle that held his goods used for bandages and medicines, and went to the side of the downed man. He looked at the break, gave a quick look at the rest of the man, saw some other scrapes but nothing serious, and turned to work on the leg. He doused the leg with water from his water bag, wiped it clean, and recognizing the need for a splint, looked around for something to use. Beside the man lay a quiver with four arrows, and Gabe grinned, knowing the value of the arrows, but also the need for the splint. *Oh well, I'll save the heads and fletching for him to use later,* he thought, and stood to fetch the arrows.

When he finished, he sat back and looked at the man. Gabe was certain he was Omaha, long hair, a top-knot with a feather, now broken, buckskin leggings, breech cloth and beaded tunic and an *akon-*

da-bpa or leather bracer on his wrist, used to protect against the slap of the bow string and as a sign he was a protector and provider for his people. As Gabe looked at the young man, he began to stir, moan and wince, and his eyes fluttered open.

Gabe watched him, then spoke in the language of the Omaha, a language similar to the Otoe and Osage, "Do not move. Your leg is broken," pointing to the man's leg.

The warrior looked down, tried to move, winced, and looked at Gabe, then at his dead horse. "You?" pointing to his leg.

"Yes." Gabe pointed to the circling buzzards, "We need to get you out of here." Gabe offered him a drink from his water bag and the man eagerly accepted. Then looked to Gabe as he handed the bag back, which Gabe exchanged for a strip of smoked meat.

The young man accepted, tore off a chunk and chewed, looking around as he did, seeing the horse and mule, frowned, and looked back. "I am Black Snake of the *U-mo'n-Ho'n.*" He looked at Gabe with an expectant expression.

Gabe grinned, "I am Spirit Bear, but I am a friend of the Omaha. I have met Black Cloud, White Elk Woman, Blackbird, and Running Fox."

The young man's eyes flared as he scowled, "How do you know my sister, Running Fox?"

Gabe leaned back, frowning at the young man, "You are Running Fox's brother?"

"Yes, Fox is the Shaman of my people. My father and mother have crossed over, but Blackbird is still the leader of our people." He looked at Gabe, cocked his head to the side and asked, "Fox spoke of a time that a white man saved her from an attack by a French slaver, are you that man?"

Gabe slowly grinned, dropped his head and chuckled, "That was a long time ago." He looked up at Snake and asked, "She was supposed to join with Two Crows, did she not do that?"

Snake shook his head, "She did, but he was killed in a battle with the Pawnee. Fox studied with our father who was the Holy Man of our people, now she stands in his place."

Gabe grinned, shook his head, then looked up at Snake. "So," and nodded toward the horse, "what happened here?"

"I spotted a Pawnee raiding party. I thought they were headed to my village and I rode to warn them." He nodded to the horse, "My pony stepped in a hole."

"Tell me about this raiding party, how big?" asked Gabe.

Snake flashed both hands, all fingers, three times, "This many!"

"Where were they?"

"Beyond the river," he pointed as he spoke.

Gabe glanced in the direction he indicated, knew the river to be one he had crossed and that fed the

Missouri, and known as the Platte. He looked back to Snake, "The big river that feeds the Missouri, or the little one?" he was thinking of a smaller stream, further north and not too distant from where they were, a tributary of the Platte he thought was called the Elkhorn.

"The small one," answered Snake.

Gabe asked, "Think you can ride with that?" motioning toward the leg.

"I will try."

Gabe had bound the leg tightly with wide strips of buckskin over the legging to hold it firm with the shafts from the arrows, but it would be hanging down and would be painful. But if the village were in danger, they had to be warned, even though the Pawnee could have already struck.

After Gabe hoisted the young man aboard the mule, he chuckled as he looked at him. He sat behind the packsaddle, with his leg crossed side-saddle style across the pack in front of him and did not look very comfortable. "I think that will make it easier on your leg, but it won't be an easy ride!"

The warrior nodded, motioned for Gabe to lead off, and the odd-looking pair took to the trail, Wolf in the lead. It was about two hours later when they came in sight of the big village, the mud hut lodges in the familiar circular layout, and without hesitation they rode into the village. Nothing looked amiss, they were greeted rather reservedly with the people look-

ing at the strange white man and his odd pack animal
with one of their own atop. It was obvious there had
been no attack, although the village was rather sparse
with people. Gabe had pulled the mule alongside and
asked, "So, where is everybody?"

"The hunt, it is the time of greening and many have
gone to hunt buffalo," answered Snake.

"Why didn't you go?" asked Gabe.

"I was on a vision quest. I am to stay with the village, hunt for the grandfathers and grandmothers."

Gabe slowly nodded his head, motioned for Snake
to direct him where to go, and the young man motioned him onward. As they neared the center of the
village, several youngsters and others had followed
them, more out of curiosity about the wolf than
anything, but when they stopped, Snake called out,
"Running Fox! I brought a friend!"

Gabe glanced from Snake to the lodge before them
and watched as the blanket at the entry was pushed
aside and a figure emerged, attired in a long beaded
buckskin tunic, matching moccasins, and holding a
coup stick with totems dangling. She stood, shield-
ing her eyes from the glare of the sun, and saw the
bearded white man aboard the buckskin, her brother
trying to get down from a long-eared something, and
a big black wolf that stood beside the buckskin. Her
interest went to her brother and she stepped near to
help him down, looking at his bandaged leg and then

to him, "What happened?"

"My horse hit a prairie dog hole. But that is not important, there is a raiding party of Pawnee near, they could be coming this way!"

She frowned at him, "No, they were driven away this morning. The hunting party with Weasel Child sent them away with several dead." She frowned and asked with a nod to the man behind her, "Who is your friend."

Snake grinned as he leaned against the mule, "He is not my friend, he is your friend."

Fox frowned, slowly turned, and walked around the head of the buckskin to look at the man that sat lazily in his saddle, grinning. Gabe had said nothing, just enjoying the moment, and as she shaded her eyes to look at him, she asked, "What are you called?"

He chuckled, swung a leg over the rump of the buckskin to step down, and turned to face the woman. "I am called Spirit Bear, but you know me by another name."

Fox's eyes flared, a smile started, and she flung her arms around Gabe as she said, "Gabe! Gabe! Gabe!" and hugged him tight. He returned the embrace and then they pushed apart to look at one another, both grinning and laughing with tears filling their eyes.

"You haven't changed a bit! You're still as beautiful as ever!" said Gabe.

Fox smiled, and answered, "You do not look the same!" rubbing her hands at her chin to indicate his chin whiskers.

***

He spent the night with the Omaha, renewing old acquaintances and sharing remembrances with this incredibly special friend. She had been the Shaman for the people for two years and would spend the rest of her life in this position. She would never take another mate, because of her commitment to her people, but she was very happy.

"I'm proud of you, Fox. You will do well for your people, I'm certain," said Gabe as he swung aboard the buckskin. "Your people are fortunate to have such a woman as their Shaman."

They had embraced and parted with tears, but now he looked down at this woman from his past, remembering their first meeting, and said, "Ezra will be happy to hear you're doing well."

"If you or Ezra are ever in the land of the Omaha, I will look for you and want you to stay with us," she said as she put her hand on his knee. They both remembered how they almost became a couple, but fate was not to allow it, and now they both had different lives, but fulfilling lives, nevertheless. As he rode from the village, he lifted a hand in goodbye and turned away, bound for the north country and a reunion with Ezra and Grey Dove, and their new addition.

30 / Contact

"The Spanish Governor General that revoked Choteau's license there at the Kansas River, I think his name was Sebastian Calvo de la Puerta somethin', well, he made a deal with Choteau. Said he could have a post with the Ponca if we could make it that far," drolled Phillipe as he sat with the tin in his lap, eating the beans and biscuits prepared by Nigel. He looked at Gabe, "Course, I was thinkin' it'd be better to have a post with the Assiniboine, the way you talked about 'em, but . . ." he took another big bite, chewing on the tidbits of meat. It was fresh bear meat, taken by Gabe just the day before when he stumbled across a big black boar tearing at a standing dead pine that had a beehive in the hollow trunk. When the bear turned toward him, face covered with honey and a mask of bees, Gabe was startled and started to leave well enough alone, but the bear, unable to do much with the bees, decided to take it out on Gabe and the animals and dropped to all fours to charge. The buckskin had shifted so quickly to the side, she left Gabe hanging in mid-air, hand on the stock of the Ferguson as he snatched it from the scabbard and landed on his rump. But he rolled to the side and the bear, somewhat blinded by the bees, missed on his first charge, giving Gabe just enough time to come to one knee, cock the Ferguson and lower the boom on the bear.

"So, what are you sayin'?" asked Gabe, wondering where the conversation was going.

"Well, we did some tradin' with the Omaha, and the Poncas, well, it was alright. But, you said there's several different bands of Sioux," he paused, looking to Gabe for a response.

Gabe nodded, "Yeah, there's Yankton to the east, Miniconjou and Two Kettle to the north and west, Arikara and Teton Sioux also to the north and west."

"Yeah, and that's a lot of different natives to trade with, and most of 'em are out on their spring hunt, which would give us time to build us a post."

"So, you're thinkin' of stayin' hereabouts?" queried Gabe.

"That's right. What do you think?" asked Phillipe.

"I haven't had much to do with the Sioux. I know they are not much different than other native peoples, there's good and bad with all. But I think if you deal honestly and fairly with them, they'll treat you right. But, you try to take advantage, cheat 'em, or do 'em dirty in any way, then you might as well pack up and make a run for it. They won't stand for that kind of treatment."

"Good advice. I'm gonna think about it, maybe camp here for a few days, let you scout around for us and lay in some meat, then decide."

Gabe looked at the man, nodded, and finished his food, set the tin down, filled his coffee cup, and sat back to think a little himself. They were about two, three days north of where he and Ezra had left the Ponca village when they first came to this country. They had followed the Niobrara River west into Cheyenne and Arapaho country, bearing south into the Arapahoe land. But if he stayed north, bearing due west, he should come onto the Wind River, at least the northern reaches of it before it fed into the Shoshone and the Yellowstone. He grinned at the thought, sipped his coffee and began to feel a little homesick for the mountains and his friends.

He spent the next two days bringing in meat. He bagged two deer the first morning, another that evening, two antelope and another deer the second day, and when he came into camp, bloody from his butchering, Nigel was all smiles and welcoming. "Gabe, m'boy, we be eatin' fine now!" and dispatched the assigned helpers to take the carcasses and start skinning. Gabe stepped down, led the horse and mule to the trees, stripped the gear and rubbed them down. Once the animals were tended to, he pulled his second set of buckskins from his bedroll, motioned for Wolf to follow and went to a deep pool behind an eddy of the river, and stripped down, and dove in, came up and called to Wolf who hesitated, dropping his chin on the bank, rump in the air, and finally was coaxed into the water.

When he came from the water, Phillipe was there, tossed him a blanket to dry off, and sat waiting. Gabe looked at him as he slipped on his buckskin trousers, and said, "Looks like you've decided to stay!"

Phillipe grinned, "Yes, I have. We're all tired of pushing up the river, and this is a good place, plenty of timber to build the post, game aplenty, and I like it."

"It will be an easily defended post also, what with the river behind it, good clear field of fire all around, that is if you cut the trees like you should, and if you put up a palisade, it will be good."

Phillipe stood, looking around, "You know, I hadn't thought of that, but you're right."

"Plan for the worst, hope for the best," declared Gabe, finishing dressing. He plopped down on the grass, Phillipe joining him, and added, "I don't think you'll have any trouble, but it's best to be prepared. Coming down this way last summer I saw several posts abandoned, burned, and such like, but that doesn't mean they were attacked, but . . ." he let the thought hang. The men sat silent for a moment, then Gabe said, "So, if you've decided, then I'll be headin' out come first light. It'll prob'ly take me another month or more to get where I'm goin' and," he looked to the setting sun, "It would be best to get there before winter comes."

***

He decided not to wait for first light, the moon was waxing full, the night was clear, and he was anxious. He had not ridden far the last couple days, staying closer to camp to get the meat for the men, and both the horse and mule were fresh enough. He had loaded up on fresh supplies before leaving, and the packs were full, both of provisions and supplies and trade goods, which always came in handy for making peace with restless native peoples.

It was the land of the Sioux, the Miniconjou and the Two Kettle bands, neither of whom were known for their friendly ways. A warring people by nature, the Sioux were known for the fearless warriors and Gabe was alone with no help to be found anywhere. He smiled at the thought, reveling in his solitary way, what some might call lonely, but he enjoyed the time alone. The moon gave light to the rugged grasslands, marred and marked by gullies and ridges, making the way a little challenging, but Gabe also knew the terrain offered him cover, if there were any eyes watching through the night.

For three nights, he continued west, paralleling the crooked White river, so named because of its color as it carried the runoff from the west over the volcanic ash and clay soils in the dry lands. On his fourth night, the river bore to the south, and Gabe knew it now marked the boundary between the Two Kettle Sioux and the Cheyenne, neither of which were too friendly with whites.

The terrain of the past night and this night as well was one of desolation and wasteland. The chalky white alkali and volcanic ash glared white in the moonlight, and rising ridges that stood above painted clay hills held pillars, towers, and ridges that rose as spectres in the dim light of night. He stopped and gave the animals a drink, using his water bag and hat as a pail, and they drank thirstily. Although the terrain he now traveled was flatter than what he had crossed earlier, it was also drier, and every footfall raised puffs of dust. He stopped again, using a wet cloth to wipe the dust from the nostrils of the buckskin and the mule. He looked to the lowering moon, knew the day was coming soon and he needed to find fresh water and shelter for the animals and himself. Wolf panted beside him and Gabe gave him a drink, and the wolf padded on, scouting the trail before them.

Gabe was remembering the previous journey, and began calculating, *If I keep to the south, I'll run into the Platte, Arapaho country, then take the Platte west to the Sweetwater and into the southern Wind River mountains. But if I turn due west, its straight across Cheyenne country, then I'll strike the Wind River, back to the mountains and home.*

He thought as he traveled, still following the White River south, and by first light, they had passed the shadows and phantoms of the dry lands and suddenly before them, the river twisted among green trees and bushes. He found a tree covered peninsula that pushed into the river and offered access to the water and shade for the camp, and he eagerly reined up and stepped down. He stripped the animals of their gear, led them to the water and a backwater pool offered water that was clear enough to see bottom and they drank. He led them further into the water, washed them down to rid them of the chalky dust that would get under the saddles and blankets and rub them raw. Wolf splashed into the water, bellied down and let the current rinse over him as he watched Gabe with the horse and mule. Gabe also stripped off his buckskins, shook them out, rinsed them clean and tossed them on the bank as he sat in the cool water to refresh himself. He rinsed his hair and beard, and the entire bunch left the water together.

They rested well throughout the day, although Wolf and Gabe slept somewhat fitfully, stirring at the least sound, whether from the wind or cracking timbers. But as evening approached, Gabe was eager to be gone from the place that seemed to have spooks and haunts, and with a handful of smoked meat, his water bag full, he gigged the buckskin to the trail.

But they had been on the trail less than an hour,

dusk was beginning to settle and the waning moon was showing its face in the eastern sky, when a scream from his left jerked Gabe's head around to see a bunch, maybe three or four, of warriors coming toward him, their horses at a run. They were waving lances and shields in the air, as they slapped legs to their mounts.

Gabe needed no encouragement as he also slapped leather to the buckskin, shouting, "Let's go, girl!" and the mare stretched out her head, dug her heels deep and launched into a full run, pulling the lead rope of the mule taut and urging him to follow. Gabe lay low on the horse's neck, mane whipping his face, as the mare stretched out into a steady ground eating gait. With one glance over his shoulder, he saw the four pursuers coming on, and he snatched his pistol from his belt, and with no hope of hitting any one of them, he snapped off a shot their direction. He quickly twisted the barrels and cocked the second hammer, turned in his saddle and with an off-handed aim, dropped the hammer again. The pistol bucked, spat smoke and lead, and did no harm. Still they came, and the screaming war cries sounded as if they had been encouraged.

He realized the Indians, probably Two Kettle Sioux, thought he only had at most two shots, and would now be defenseless. He grinned, stuffed the Bailes over/ under back in his belt and lifted the first of the saddle pistols. He cocked one hammer, slowed the buckskin just a little, and turned, lay the pistol in the crook of his elbow, and fired. He watched and saw one of the four flinch, grab at his horse's mane, and struggle to stay aboard. Gabe cocked the second hammer and fired again, and saw the rest of the group rein up, shake their shields and lances at him and screamed their war cries, as Gabe turned and slapped legs to the buckskin again and made tracks across the flats beside the river.

Gabe knew his animals were fresh and those of the Sioux had probably been ridden all day, whether on a hunt or raid, and they would not pursue any further. He grinned at the memory of their shouted taunts and war cries as he rode away. He slowed the buckskin, turned in his saddle to search his back trail and satisfied there was no pursuit, he pointed the mare to the river bank and reined up. As the animals drank their fill of the water, now running clear and slow, he reloaded his pistols and returned them to their place. And made his decision, he would continue south until he came to the Platte, then go west to the mountains.

31 / Mountains

Three days out from his runaway with the Sioux, he came to the headwaters, such as they were, more of a dry creek bed, of the White River. Following the White as it bore south southwest, brought him closer to the Niobrara and the moon had waned enough to entice him to travel by day. He stopped for a short camp, fixed coffee, and ate the last of his cornmeal biscuits, and with the horse and mule tethered near a cluster of piñon, he stretched out beside Wolf and took a bit of a snooze. But the warm sun on his face by late morning roused him, the shade having retreated close to the trees, and he loaded his gear and set out for the Niobrara.

By dusk, he was at the headwaters of the Niobrara and the marsh and bog among the willows were little to look at, but he bore to the southwest a few more miles and found a suitable camp on the north side of a timbered ridge that rose two to three hundred feet above the plains floor. At least it was shelter from the howling winds that pushed down from the northwest. Three days of looking at the mountains off his left shoulder, brought him alongside the meandering North Platte River, and he followed it as it bent to the south, cutting through the rolling hills and deep canyons to bring him to the big solitary stone that reminded him of a giant turtle, rising over two hundred feet high and a quarter mile long, the landmark bore etchings made long ago by ancient travelers, mostly petroglyphs made by natives, but there was also the carved image of a Spanish cross. It was here he joined the Sweetwater and pushed on through the narrow cut, having to take to the water to make it through, but finally he was into the Sweetwater basin, and travel would be easy, for now, on a clear morning he could see the distant Wind River mountains.

Four days of dusty travel following the Sweetwater with nothing but sage, bunch grass, greasewood, rabbit brush and cacti on his left, the meandering Sweetwater that held the grass and willows close, on his right. Beyond the little river, rolling and ragged hills followed as shadows of long forgotten passersby. But always before him, the southern end of the magnificent Wind River mountains.

The morning of his fifth day in the great basin, he turned his back on the flats and pushed northwest, the red clay of the long canyon beckoning. It was here, in the

shelter of the grey and purple bluffs where the narrow
willow clad stream carved its way through the red clay
and cut a wide swath, leaving green in its wake as it
pointed to the mountains, here was where he first saw
Pale Otter's people. He stopped at the confluence of two
creeks, one coming from the west, the other pushing
to the north, and loosened the girths on the saddles, let
the animals graze on the fresh grass, and he prepared
to make a small hat-sized fire to brew some coffee. He
chose a site where camps had been made before and he
kicked some old charcoal to a pile, put some tinder on
top, and with flint and steel, soon had his fire going.

He took a seat on a big flat rock, looked around
the valley with the bluffs rising before him, shading
the late morning sun, and then to the long slanted
ridges with their white stone edges that accented
the muted red of the clay slopes below. The brilliant
green of summer grass and willows laid a carpet that
separated the two differing terrains, but also showed
the trail he would follow. As the coffee pot danced, he
remembered their first time here, and the first time he
saw the people of Pale Otter, Nanawu and Chochoco,
her aunt and her son. He had often wondered why
they had not met at this first visit, but it was a short
time and they left after the first day. He smiled at the
thought of meeting Pale Otter sooner and wondered
if his reaction would have been the same. *Of course
it would!* he thought, knowing that every glimpse of

her made him catch his breath until they were joined together in marriage, and even then whenever he looked at her he wondered how he could have been so lucky as to have her as his wife.

Every memory was burned deep in his mind and heart and he would treasure them always, being able to relive those moments gave him encouragement to go on, to take the next step, to ride to the next mountain. He lifted his eyes to the valley, saw a patch of tall fireweed just starting to burst out in bloom, waving their tall stalks and the bright pink blossoms, as if waving him on, and he breathed deep again as he stood to start on the trail, remembering how Otter said the flowers were waving at her, bidding her come.

It was late afternoon when he came to the Popo Agie creek, the fast rushing white water that came from the narrow cleft between the big shouldered foothills of the Wind River Mountains. He crossed the shallow stream, pushed through the willows, and took to the trail that rode the north bank and the low end of the steep sloping hills. The southern slopes on his left were covered with piñon and juniper, but those on his right, mostly bare and rocky.

The clatter of his animals' hooves on the hard packed and rocky trail echoed back and forth in the narrow canyon giving a rhythmic cadence to their movements while the roar of rapids crashing over the rocks provided the chorus of the mountain melody. The trail forced another crossing of the creek, just below the pool where the water emerged from its underground lair. Another half mile and the stream chuckled its way into the rocky face of the mountain and retreated from sight under the cliff. But Gabe followed the stream another two miles to the big boulder bluff that crowded the water into the narrows as Gabe took to the shoulder hugging trail around the bulbous point.

Another half-mile and the trail and stream parted ways, the stream cascading through the narrow rocky defile, tumbling over a series of falls as its crashing waters roared from the canyon. The trail shifted higher on the shoulder and rose to point into the mouth of a hanging valley. Gabe reined up as the trail rose above the mouth of the valley to perch atop a rocky knob that gave a promontory overlooking the entire valley, the granite tipped peaks beyond, and the big stony knob that marked the place of their cabin. He stepped down, stood beside the buckskin, reached down to run his fingers through the scruff of Wolf's neck, and then dropped to one knee and drew the big black beast close beside him.

"We're home boy, we're home." He stood, looking and longing to see some sign of life, but there was none. It appeared just as it did the first time they saw this valley, green and inviting, and empty. He sighed heavily, looked at Wolf, then swung aboard the buckskin, "C'mon, let's go see if the cabin's still standin'!" He gigged the buckskin forward and they followed the trail through the scrub oak and grass up the long slope toward the bluff. The rocky slopes parted, and the trail pushed through the tall brush that was as high as Gabe's belt as he sat in the saddle.

Suddenly the buckskin stopped, lifted her head high, ears pricked and whinnied. Gabe felt the belly of the mare bounce as she whinnied again, and in the distance came an answering neigh. Gabe stood in his stirrups, but saw nothing, and nudged the mare forward with his heels. Wolf took off at a run and Gabe saw the black fur disappear between two low rising knolls. He urged the buckskin on, but the lead rope from the mule pulled taut and the mule stopped, lifted his head, long ears pointing, and stared ahead. Coming through the low point between the knolls was a high-stepping black horse, head high, long mane flying, and tail lifted like a flag.

Gabe grinned, whistled and the stallion came at a run, Wolf right behind him. Gabe jumped to the ground, dropped the reins of the buckskin, and greeted Ebony with a hug around his neck. The stallion lifted him off the ground, just as happy to see Gabe as the man was to see him. When Gabe gained his feet, he rubbed his face against the face of the black, "Boy, it is good to see you!" and hugged his neck again.

He stepped back, and looked behind the stallion, searching for anyone or anything else, but the stallion was alone. Gabe grabbed the reins of the buckskin, and walking beside Ebony, with Wolf beside him, started toward the cabin, or the log fronted overhang that answered to the name of cabin. This was the home they built for their first winter in the wilderness, and the cavern served them well. They had split the space into a stable on one side and their living quarters on the other. With four rooms, two bedrooms, a main room, and a kitchen/eating area, it had been a pleasant home for the first winter Gabe and Ezra enjoyed with their wives, Pale Otter and Grey Dove.

As he rounded the knoll, his first look at the cabin thrilled him. It looked exactly like they left it, but he was hoping to see Ezra and Dove. He stood looking at the cabin, and his memory painted the image of Otter, standing in the doorway, beckoning him homeward. He shook his head, lifted his eyes again, turned to look around, and noticed a thin wisp of smoke snaking upward from beyond the shoulder of the knoll below the cabin. He frowned, glanced around nearby, and started walking toward the rocky knob, following a familiar foot trail they had traveled many times before when the summer camp of the Shoshone nestled in the valley below.

As he neared, the tips of tipi poles started showing, more thin spirals of smoke pointed into the clear sky, and Gabe quickened his step. He stopped atop the knoll, looking at the sprawling village below, looking just like it did when Dove and Otter were there with their people, the summer before they were joined. He smiled, watching the usual activity of the village, children chasing a hoop with sticks, youngsters trying their skill with bows and blunted arrows, women scraping hides that were stretched on racks, men scraping the straight shafts that would become arrows, and cook fires flaming under hanging pots. It was a pleasing sight, but as he looked, he saw no one familiar, or at least, he did not see Ezra or Dove.

He dropped to one knee, his arm over the neck of Wolf as he spoke, "So, where are they. . ." but he was stopped as Wolf whirled around and took off toward the cabin. Gabe stood, turned, and saw two riders coming from behind the big stone bluff, familiar riders. They reined up at the sight of the ground tied buckskin and mule, Ebony standing beside the buckskin.

Gabe grinned and started walking back to the cabin, watching Ezra step down then help Dove with her cradleboard on her back. Gabe walked close, stood watching and grinning, and when Ezra turned around, the two men gave one another a bear hug, slapping each other on the back and laughing all the while. When Ezra released him, Gabe stepped to Dove to give her a hug, although it was a little awkward with the baby carrier still strapped on, but they managed. He stepped back, "Well, look at you. Quite a family! So, what's the little one's name?"

Ezra chuckled, looked at Gabe, "Doesn't have one yet. That's your job!"

Gabe frowned, looked from Ezra to Dove and back, "I don't understand. How is it my job?"

"It is always the responsibility of the uncle to give the little one their first name. Since you are the husband of her sister, that makes you the uncle, so, what's his name?" said Ezra.

Gabe grinned, shaking his head, "So, you have a son! I'm mighty proud of you two! But, it might take me a while to come up with a suitable name."

Ezra looked past him at the mule and buckskin, "How 'bout we get you unloaded and settled in and then maybe you can come up with a suitable name for my son."

Gabe nodded, turned to join Ezra as they stripped the packs from the mule and saddle from the buckskin. Dove went into the cabin as the men worked outside. Gabe was muttering, "Elijah, Elisha, Paul, Matthew, Jabez," he paused as he stripped the saddle from the mare, dropping it beside the packs, "Badger, Wolf, Beaver," he heard a hawk cry from on high, "Hawk, Sparrow, Eagle, Woodpecker."

"Don't you even think of it!" demanded Ezra when he heard the last, "Even though he can be noisy and wake us up, he ain't no woodpecker!"

Gabe chuckled, "I know most little ones would deserve the name of skunk, but . . ." and the two friends chuckled together as they picked up the gear to carry it into the cabin. As they stepped inside, the smells of food cooking and coffee boiling filled the room and Gabe paused, saddle in hand, smiled, and said, "It's good to be home!"

Available Soon:
Shoshone Summer (Stonecroft Saga 8)

What started as a joyous reunion of friends, soon became one of the most challenging periods of their lives. Chosen as scouts for the Kuccuntikka village of the Shoshone for their trek to the grand encampment of the Shoshone, their encounter with the scouts from the Tukkutikka band would set them on a different course altogether. When Gabe meets the war leader of the other band, he is challenged at every turn by the woman warrior, his equal on every count. But when they are attacked by Blackfoot, a battle rages...

When a raiding party of Hidatsa warriors strike another band of Shoshone, an old friend, the war leader of the Agaideka Shoshone, asks Gabe and Ezra to join in the vengeance party to rescue the five captive girls, one of whom is his niece known as Sacajawea. But raiding Blackfoot and Hidatsa war parties were not the only challenges for the two explorers. When a jealous Shoshone warrior tries to take the place of the woman warrior war leader and seeks vengeance, the fight rages with both the war leader known as Cougar Woman and her new mate, Spirit Bear – also known as Gabe Stonecroft.

ABOUT THE AUTHOR

Born and raised in Colorado into a family of ranchers and cowboys, B.N. Rundell is the youngest of seven sons. Juggling bull riding, skiing, and high school, graduation was a launching pad for a hitch in the Army Paratroopers. After the army, he finished his college education in Springfield, MO, and together with his wife and growing family, entered the ministry as a Baptist preacher.

Together, B.N. and Dawn raised four girls that are now married and have made them proud grandparents. With many years as a successful pastor and educator, he retired from the ministry and followed in the footsteps of his entrepreneurial father and started a successful insurance agency, which is now in the hands of his trusted nephew. He has also been a successful audiobook narrator and has recorded many books for several award-winning authors. Now finally realizing his life-long dream, B.N. has turned his efforts to writing a variety of books, from children's picture books and young adult adventure books, to the historical fiction and western genres.

Printed in Great Britain
by Amazon

22298598R00162